Welcome to your new home ...

Zac felt the crunch as his waverunner hit the reef, and then he was flying though the air. He stared dumbly down as the water rushed up to meet him.

He landed hard, branches of coral slicing through his skin as his fall shattered the lacy, delicate structures. The water closed over his head. Trying not to cry out, he opened his eyes, and watched in horror as a thin, dark tendril emerged from a broken stump of coral and wrapped around his wrist. Then he did scream as the tendril stabbed into his forearm, leaving a long black barb embedded beneath the skin. He began to choke. He couldn't breathe.

He was going to drown.

TALES FROM THE WONDER ZONE

Stardust
•
Explorer
•
Orbiter
•
Odyssey

More Original Science Fiction
from Trifolium Books Inc.

**Packing Fraction
& Other Tales of Science
and Imagination**

Odyssey

Edited by
Julie E. Czerneda

Illustrated by
Jean-Pierre Normand

Trifolium Books Inc.
A Fitzhenry & Whiteside Company

© 2004 Trifolium Books Inc.
First Printing of the following:
Special Introduction © 2004 Greg Bear, Jigsaw © 2004 Douglas Smith,
Skeeters © 2004 MT O'Shaughnessy, Tides of Change © 2004 Sarah Jane
Elliott, source material © 2004 Laura Anne Gilman, To Feast on Royal Jelly
© 2004 Francine P. Lewis, Treasures © 2004 Annette Griessman, Defining
an Elephant © 2004 Peter Watts.

We acknowledge the financial support of the Government of Canada through
the book Publishing Industry Development Program (BPIDP) for our publishing
activities.

Canadian Cataloguing in Publication Data
Odyssey / edited by Julie E. Czerneda;
illustrated by Jean-Pierre Normand.
(Tales from the wonder zone)
ISBN 1-55244-080-X

1. Children's stories, Canadian (English) 2. Children's stories, American.
3. Science fiction, Canadian (English) 4. Science fiction, American. I.
Czerneda, Julie, 1955- II. Normand, Jean-Pierre III. Series.

PS8323.S3O39 2004   jC813'.08762089282   C2003-906696-7

Trifolium Books Inc.
195 Allstate Parkway,
Markham, Ontario L3R 4T8
godwit@fitzhenry.ca   www.fitzhenry.ca

Cover Design and Illustrations: Jean-Pierre Normand
Text Composition: Fortunato Design Inc.

Printed and bound in Canada
9 8 7 6 5 4 3 2 1

Dedications

Julie E. Czerneda: To Hal Clement (aka Harry Stubbs), who gifted us with his sense of wonder and generous spirit. To Roxanne Hubbard and Isaac Szpindel, for all their help. To Sharon Fitzhenry, for sharing the vision. To the contributors and their amazing imaginations. To Greg Bear, my special thanks, for his wonderful introduction and unceasing support. And, as always, to Jean-Pierre Normand, who brings words to life.

Douglas Smith: To my Dad, who is battling Alzheimer's. His memories have become like the puzzle in my story — pieces from a jigsaw, a fragmented picture that he can't always recall. For now, thank god, my face and name are still on one of those pieces.

MT O'Shaughnessy: Happily the list is too long to squeeze in. So thanks to all, and: Julie, Ruth, and Wayne.

Sarah Jane Elliott: For Nancy Clark and Deborah McLennan, who encouraged both the biologist and the writer. Sometimes all we need is a push in the right direction.

Laura Anne Gilman: For James, who demands — and gets — results.

Francine P. Lewis: To Dr. J. Fullard and Dr. G. Pollack, for teaching me to see the world and beyond. To my family and friends, thank you for your love and support — I'm finally getting "on with it."

Annette Griessman: For Alex and Kayla — my treasures.

Peter Watts: For everyone with tied (or severed) tubes. 6.2 billion is more than enough.

CONTENTS

A Special Introduction by Greg Bear   ix

Jigsaw by Douglas Smith   1

Skeeters by MT O'Shaughnessy   27

Tides of Change by Sarah Jane Elliott   51

To Feast on Royal Jelly by Francine P. Lewis   75

source material by Laura Anne Gilman   98

Treasures by Annette Griessman   101

Defining an Elephant by Peter Watts   115

A Special Introduction by Greg Bear

Curious? Like to discover new things?

Have I got a game for you! It's infinitely long and infinitely wide, but it fits on a page. It's made up of secret signs and coded messages: the alphabet. It's magic, because rearranging the secret signs creates entire worlds filled with incredible people and creatures. Nobody knows what it can do but you. No one else will play this game the way you do. They can't.

They're not you.

Open this book and dive in. Visit reefs that speak and appoint guardians; an all-consuming fire that lives; travel to other worlds and meet beings who are like you, but not, not really like you at all. What can you learn from them? What can you teach them in return?

The game begins —

But wait! You're looking around the room, watching people watching you. Is it embarrassing? Are you afraid that others might think you're stupid, or silly? Because you're interested in things besides clothes and celebrities and cars and fashion magazines, because you like exploring what you don't understand, and seeing and touching?

I don't think so. You've come this far.

The game is called science fiction. It's where all the knowledge in the world lies down to relax and dream and tell stories. The game has chosen *you*. Don't you feel it? Kind of spooky, right, but you knew it all along!

So relax. Come dream with us. Read, then make up your own stories. Explore your own worlds. You are bigger and stronger on the inside than the outside.

And the game is bigger than you and me. It lasts a lifetime, you see.

Or longer.

Greg Bear

Greg Bear is the Hugo and Nebula Award-winning author of *Darwin's Children* and *The Collected Stories of Greg Bear*

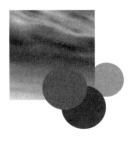

Jigsaw

by Douglas Smith

Still in shock, Cassie Morant slumped in the cockpit of the empty hopper, staring at the two viewplates before her.

In one, the planet Griphus, a blue, green and brown marble wrapped in belts of cloud, grew smaller. Except for the shape of its land masses, it could have been Earth.

But it wasn't. Griphus was an alien world, light-years from Sol System.

A world where nineteen of her shipmates were going to die.

And one of them was Davey.

In the other viewplate, the segmented, tubular hull of the orbiting Earth wormship, the *Johannes Kepler*, grew larger. Cassie tapped a command, and the ship's vector appeared, confirming her fears.

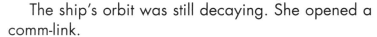

The ship's orbit was still decaying. She opened a comm-link.

"Hopper Two to the *Kepler*. Requesting docking clearance," she said.

Silence. Then a male voice crackled over the speaker, echoing cold and metallic in the empty shuttle.

"Acknowledged, Hopper Two. You are clear to dock, segment beta four, port nine."

Cassie didn't recognize the voice, but that wasn't surprising. The *Kepler* held the population of a small city, and Cassie was something of a loner. But she had no trouble identifying the gruff rumble she heard next.

"Pilot of hopper, identify yourself. This is Captain Theodor."

Cassie took a breath. "Sir, this is Dr. Cassandra Morant, team geologist."

Pause. "Where's team leader Stockard?" Theodor asked.

Davey. "Sir, the rest of the surface team was captured by the indigenous tribe inhabiting the extraction site. The team is..." Cassie stopped, her throat constricting.

"Morant?"

She swallowed. "They're to be executed at sunrise."

Another pause.

"Did you get the berkelium?" Theodor finally asked.

Cassie fought her anger. Theodor wasn't being heartless. The team below was secondary to the thousands on the ship.

"Just a core sample, sir," she said. "But it confirms that the deposit's there."

Theodor swore. "Dr. Morant, our orbit decays in under twenty hours. Report immediately after docking to brief the command team." Theodor cut the link.

Cassie stared at the huge wormship, suddenly hating it, hating its strangeness. *Humans would never build something like that*, she thought.

Consisting of hundreds of torus rings strung along a central axis like donuts on a stick, the ship resembled a giant metallic worm. A dozen rings near the middle were slowly rotating, providing the few inhabited sections with an artificial gravity.

Thousands of us, and we barely fill a fraction of it, she thought. *It wasn't meant for us. We shouldn't be here.*

Humans had just begun to explore their solar system, when Max Bremer and his crew had found the wormships, three of them, outside the orbit of Pluto.

Abandoned? Lost? Or left to be found?

Found by the ever-curious, barely-out-of-the-trees man-apes of Earth. Found with charted wormholes in Sol System. Found with still-only-partly-translated, we-think-this-button-does-this libraries and databases, and we-can't-fix-it-so-it-better-never-break technology. Incredibly ancient yet perfectly functioning Wormer technology.

Wormers. The inevitable name given to Earth's unknown alien benefactors.

4

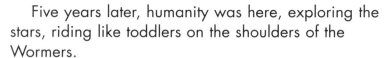

Five years later, humanity was here, exploring the stars, riding like toddlers on the shoulders of the Wormers.

But Cassie no longer wanted to be here. She wished she was back on Earth, safely cocooned in her apartment, with Vivaldi playing, lost in one of her jigsaw puzzles.

She shifted uncomfortably in the hopper seat. Like every Wormer chair, like the ship itself, it almost fit a human. But not quite.

It's like forcing a piece to fit in a jigsaw, she thought. It's a cheat, and in the end, the picture is wrong. Humans shouldn't be here. We forced ourselves into a place in the universe where we don't fit. We cheated, and we've been caught. And now we're being punished.

For they faced a puzzle that threatened the entire ship. She'd had a chance to solve it on the planet.

And she'd failed.

Cassie hugged herself, trying to think. She was good at puzzles, but this one had a piece missing. She thought back over events since they'd arrived through the wormhole four days ago. The answer had to be there…

Four days ago, Cassie had sat in her quarters on the *Kepler*, hunched over a jigsaw puzzle covering her desk. The desk, like anything Wormer, favored unbroken flowing contours, the seat sweeping up to chair back wrapping around to desk surface. Viewplates on the curved walls showed telescopic shots of Griphus. The walls and ceiling glowed softly.

Lieutenant David Stockard, Davey to Cassie, lay on her bunk watching her.

"Don't you get tired of jigsaws?" he asked.

She shrugged. "They relax me. It's my form of meditation. Besides, I'm doing my homework."

Davey rolled off the bunk. She watched him walk over, wondering again what had brought them together. If she could call what they had being "together" — sometimes friendship, sometimes romance, sometimes not-talking-to-each-other.

They seemed a case study in "opposites attract." She was a scientist, and Davey was military. She was dark, short, and slim, while he was fair, tall, and broad. She preferred spending her time quietly, reading, listening to classical music — and doing jigsaw puzzles. Davey always had to be active.

But the biggest difference lay in their attitudes to the Wormers. Davey fervently believed that the alien ships were meant to be found by humans, that the Universe wanted them to explore the stars.

To Cassie, the Universe wasn't telling them everything it knew. She felt that they didn't understand Wormer technology enough to be risking thousands of lives.

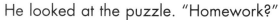

He looked at the puzzle. "Homework?"

"I printed a Mercator projection of topographic scans of Griphus onto plas-per, and the computer cut it into a jigsaw."

The puzzle showed the planet's two major continents, which Dr. Xu, head geologist and Cassie's supervisor, had dubbed Manus and Pugnus. *Hand and fist.* The western continent, Pugnus, resembled a clenched fist and forearm, punching across an ocean at Manus, which resembled an open hand, fingers and thumb curled ready to catch the fist. Colored dots, each numbered, speckled the map.

"What are the dots?" Davey asked.

"Our shopping list. Deposits of rare minerals. That is, if you believe Wormer archives and Wormer scanners —"

"Cassie, let's not start—" Davey said.

"Davey, these ships are at least ten thousand years old—"

"With self-healing nanotech—" Davey replied.

"That we don't understand—"

"Cassie..." Davey sighed.

She glared, then folded her arms. "Fine."

Davey checked the time on his per-comm unit. "Speaking of homework, Trask wants surface team rescue procedures by oh-eight-hundred. Gotta go." He kissed Cassie and left.

Cassie bit back a comment that this was a scientific, not a military, expedition. The likely need for Trask's "procedures" was low in her opinion.

She would soon change her mind.

An hour later, Cassie was walking along the busy outer corridor of the ring segment assigned to the science team. Suddenly, the ship shuddered, throwing Cassie and others against one curving wall.

The ship lurched again, and the light from the glowing walls blinked out. People screamed. Cassie stumbled and fell. And kept falling, waiting for the impact against the floor that never came, until she realized what had happened.

The ring's stopped rotating, she thought. *We've lost artificial gravity.*

She floated in darkness for maybe thirty minutes, bumping into others, surrounded by whispers, shouts, and sobbing. Suddenly, the lights flicked back on. Cassie felt gravity returning like an invisible hand tugging at her guts, followed by a sudden heaviness in her limbs. Hitting the floor, she rolled then rose on shaky legs. People stood dazed, looking like scattered pieces in a jigsaw that before had been a coherent picture of normality.

What's happened? she thought.

The intercom broke through the rising babble of conversations. "The following personnel report immediately to port six, segment beta four for surface team detail." Twenty names followed. One was Davey's.

One was hers. *What was going on?*

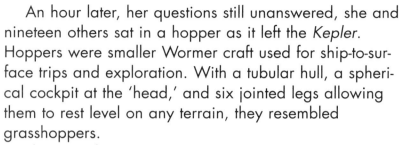

An hour later, her questions still unanswered, she and nineteen others sat in a hopper as it left the *Kepler*. Hoppers were smaller Wormer craft used for ship-to-surface trips and exploration. With a tubular hull, a spherical cockpit at the 'head,' and six jointed legs allowing them to rest level on any terrain, they resembled grasshoppers.

The team faced each other in two rows of seats in the main cabin. Cassie only knew two others besides Davey. Manfred Mubuto, balding, dark and round, was their xeno-anthropologist. Liz Branson, with features as sharp as her sarcasm, was their linguist. Four were marines. But the rest, over half the team, were mining techs. *Why?*

Davey addressed them. She'd never seen him so serious.

"The *Kepler's* power loss resulted from the primary fuel cell being purged. Engineering is working to swap cells, but that requires translating untested Wormer procedures. We may need to replenish the cell, which means extracting berkelium from Griphus for processing."

That's why I'm here, Cassie thought. Berkelium, a rare trans-uranium element, was the favored Wormer energy source. It had never been found on Earth, only manufactured. Her analysis of Griphus had shown possible deposits.

"Like every planet found via the wormholes," Davey said, "Griphus is incredibly Earth-like: atmosphere, gravity, humanoid populations—"

Liz interrupted. "We purged a fuel cell? Who screwed up?"

Davey reddened. "That's not relevant—"

"Operator error, I hear," Manfred said. "A tech misread Wormer symbols on a panel, punched an incorrect sequence—"

Liz swore. "I knew it! We're like kids trying to fly Daddy's flitter—"

Cassie started to agree, but Davey cut them off.

"We've no time for rumors," he snapped, looking at Cassie, Liz, and Manfred. "Our orbit decays in three days. I remind you that this team's under my command — including science personnel."

Manfred nodded. Liz glared, but said nothing.

Davey tapped the computer pad on his seat. A holo of Griphus appeared. "Dr. Morant, please locate the berkelium."

Cassie almost laughed at being called "Dr. Morant" by Davey, but then she caught his look. She tapped some keys, and two red dots blinked onto the holo, one in the ocean mid-way between Pugnus and Manus, and another offshore of Manus. The second site was circled.

"Wormer sensors show two sites. I've circled my recommendation," Cassie said.

"Why not the other site?" a mining tech asked.

A network of lines appeared, making the planet's surface look like a huge jigsaw puzzle.

"As on Earth," Cassie said, "the lithosphere or planetary crust of Griphus is broken into tectonic plates, irregular sections ranging from maybe fifteen kilometers thick under oceans to a hundred under continents. This shows the plate pattern on Griphus.

"Plates float on the denser, semi-molten asthenosphere, the upper part of the mantle. At 'transform' boundaries, they slide along each other, as in the San Andreas Fault on Earth. At 'convergent' boundaries, they collide, forming mountains such as the Himalayas."

A line splitting the ocean between Pugnus and Manus glowed yellow. The line also ran through the other berkelium site.

"But at 'divergent' boundaries," Cassie continued, "such as this mid-oceanic trench, magma pushes up from the mantle, creating new crust, forcing the plates apart. The other site is deep in the trench, below our sub's crush depth."

Davey nodded. "So we hit the site offshore of Manus. Any indigenous population along that coast?"

"Yes," Manfred said. "From orbital pictures, they appear tribal, agrarian, definitely pre-industrial. Some large stone structures and primitive metal-lurgy."

"Then defending ourselves shouldn't be a problem." Davey patted the stinger on his belt. The Wormer weapon was non-lethal, temporarily disrupting voluntary muscular control.

"Could we try talking before we shoot them?" Liz said.

11

Davey just smiled. "Which brings us to communication, Dr. Branson."

Liz sighed. "Wormer translator units need a critical mass of vocabulary, syntax, and context samples to learn a language. Given the time we have, I doubt they'll help much."

"With any luck, we won't need them," Davey said. "We'll locate the deposit, send in the mining submersible, and be out before they know we're there."

Looking around her, Cassie guessed that no one felt lucky.

The hopper landed on the coast near the offshore deposit. The team wore light body suits and breathing masks to prevent ingesting anything alien to human immune systems.

Cassie stepped onto a broad beach of gray sand lapped by an ocean too green for Earth, under a sky a touch too blue. The beach ran up to a forest of trees whose black trunks rose twenty meters in the air. Long silver leaves studded each trunk, glinting like sword blades in the sun. She heard a high keening that might have been birds or wind in the strange trees.

Southwards, the beach ran into the distance. But to the north, it ended at a cliff rising up to a low mesa. Cassie walked over to Davey, who was overseeing the marines unloading the submersible and drilling equipment.

"Cool, eh?" he said, looking around them.

She pointed at the mesa. "That's cooler to a rock nut."

He looked up the beach. "Okay. But keep your per-comm on."

Cassie nodded and set out. The cliff was an hour's walk. Cassie didn't mind, enjoying the exercise and strange surroundings. She took pictures of the rock strata, and climbed to get samples at different levels. Then she walked back.

They captured Cassie just as she was wondering why the hopper seemed deserted. The natives appeared so quickly and silently, they seemed to rise from the sand. Cassie estimated there were about forty of them, all remarkably human, but taller, with larger eyes, longer noses, and greenish skin. All were male, bare-chested, wearing skirts woven from sword-blade tree leaves, and leather sandals.

They led Cassie to stand before two women. One was dressed as the men but with a headdress of a coppery metal. The other was older and wore a cape of cloth and feathers. Her head was bare, her hair long and white. Beside them, pale but unharmed, stood Liz Branson, flanked by two warriors.

The older woman spoke to Liz in a sing-song melodic language. Cassie saw that the linguist wore a translator earplug. Liz sat down, motioning Cassie to do the same. The male warriors sat circling them. The two native women remained standing.

Cassie realized she was trembling. "What happened?"

Liz grimaced. "We've stepped in it big time. The

Chadorans — our captors — believe a sacred object called 'the third one' lies underwater here. Only a priestess may enter these waters. When our techs launched the sub, the natives ambushed us from the trees with blowguns. They grabbed the techs when they surfaced."

"Where's Davey?" Cassie asked, then added, "...and everyone?"

"Taken somewhere. They seemed okay."

"Why not you too?"

"The tribe's matriarchal," Liz said. "The old woman is Cha-kay, their chief. The younger one, Pre-nah, is their priestess. Because I'm female and knew their language, Cha-kay assumed I was our leader. But I said you were."

"You what?" Cassie cried.

"Cassie, we need someone they'll respect," Liz said, her face grim. "That means a female who didn't defile the site. That means you."

"God, Liz — wait, how can you talk to them?"

Liz frowned. "It's weird. The translator produced understandable versions within minutes, pulling from Wormer archives of other worlds. That implies all those languages share the same roots. The Wormers may have seeded all these worlds."

Cassie didn't care. "What can I do?"

"Convince Cha-kay to let us go."

"How?" Cassie asked.

"She wants to show you something. It's some sort of test."

"And if I fail?"

Liz handed Cassie the translator. "Then they'll kill us."

Cassie swallowed. "I won't let that happen."

They led Cassie to a long boat with a curving prow powered by a dozen rowers. Cha-kay rode in a chair near the stern, Cassie at her feet. Pre-nah and six warriors stood beside them.

They traveled up a winding river through dense jungle. Conversation was sparse, but sufficient to convince Cassie that the translator unit worked. After three hours, they landed at a clearing. Cassie climbed out, happy to move and stretch. She blinked.

Blue cubes, ranging from one to ten meters high, filled the clearing. They were hewn from stone and painted. The party walked past the cubes to a path that switch-backed up a low mountain. They began to climb.

Cassie groaned but said nothing, since the aged Cha-kay didn't seem bothered by the climb. As they went, Cassie noticed smaller cubes beside the path.

Night had fallen when they reached the top and stepped onto a tabletop of rock about eighty meters across. Cassie gasped.

A huge cube, at least fifty meters on each side nearly filled the plateau. It was blue. It was glowing.

And it was hovering a meter off the ground.

Cha-kay led Cassie to it, and Cassie received another shock. On its smooth sides, Cassie could see familiar symbols.

The artifact, whatever its purpose, was Wormer.

Cha-kay prostrated herself, telling Cassie to do the same. As she did, Cassie peeked underneath the cube. A column of pulsating blue light shone from a crevice to touch the base of the artifact at its center. Reaching down to her belt, Cassie activated her scanner. She'd check the readings later.

Rising, Cha-kay indicated a large diagram on the artifact. In it, a cube, a sphere, and a tetrahedron formed points of an equilateral triangle.

"It is a map. We are here," Cha-kay said, pointing to the cube. "The gods left three artifacts, but hid one. The third will appear when the gods return and lay their hands on the other two." Then, pointing to the outline of a hand on the artifact, Cha-kay looked at Cassie.

"Touch," she said.

With a sudden chill, Cassie understood. *They think we're the Wormers, finally returning*, she thought.

This was the test, on which the lives of her shipmates, of the entire ship, depended.

Reaching out a trembling hand, Cassie felt resistance from some invisible barrier and a warm tingling, then her hand slipped through onto the outline on the artifact.

Nothing happened.

Murmurs grew behind her. Feeling sick, Cassie looked at Cha-kay. To her surprise, the old woman smiled.

"Perhaps," Cha-kay said, "it rises even now."

Cassie understood. Cha-kay hoped to find that the

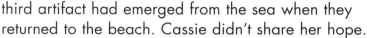

third artifact had emerged from the sea when they returned to the beach. Cassie didn't share her hope.

They spent the night there. Pretending to sleep, Cassie checked her scanner readings. They confirmed her suspicions. The column of light showed berkelium emissions. The artifact was connected to a deposit as an energy source.

The next day, a similar journey brought them to the second artifact, located on another flat mountain peak. The only difference was the artifact itself, a huge glowing red tetrahedron. Cassie again saw a column of light underneath and detected berkelium. She touched the artifact, again with no apparent effect, and the party began the trip back.

Cha-kay seemed to have grown genuinely fond of Cassie. She told Cassie how her people found the artifacts generations ago, eventually realizing that the drawing was a map. They learned to measure distances and angles, and determined that the third artifact lay in the coastal waters. Priestesses had dived there for centuries but found nothing. Still they believed.

Cassie did some calculations, and found the Chadoran estimate remarkably accurate. Still, she wondered why the Wormers would locate two artifacts in identical settings on mountain plateaus, yet place the third underwater. Perhaps the third location had subsided over the years. But her scans showed no sunken mountains off the coast.

Cassie enjoyed Cha-kay's company, but as they neared the coast, her fear grew. Cha-kay fell silent as well. As the boat reached the beach, they stood at the railing, hands clasped, scanning the waters for the third artifact.

Nothing.

Cries arose among the warriors. Pre-nah approached Cha-kay. "The strangers are false gods," the priestess said. "They must die."

Cha-kay stared across the ocean. Finally, she nodded. Cassie's legs grew weak as two warriors moved towards her.

Cha-kay raised her hand. "No. This one goes free. She did not defile the sacred place."

Pre-nah didn't look pleased, but she bowed her head.

They landed, and Cha-kay walked with Cassie to the hopper.

"When?" Cassie asked, her voice breaking.

"At sunrise, child," Cha-kay said. "I am sorry."

Cassie boarded the hopper. She engaged the auto-launch, then slumped in her seat, as the planet and her hopes grew smaller.

After docking, Cassie went immediately to the briefing room, as Captain Theodor had ordered. She quickly took a seat in one of a dozen Wormer chairs around a holo display unit. Dr. Xu gave her a worried smile.

Commander Trask glared.

Theodor cleared his throat, a rumble that brought everyone's gaze to his stocky form.

"I'll be brief. Our orbit collapses in nineteen hours. Attempts to swap fuel cells were unsuccessful. The team sent to extract the berkelium has been captured and faces execution. Only Dr. Morant escaped."

Everyone looked at Cassie. All she could think of was how she'd failed.

Theodor continued. "Dr. Morant will summarize events on the planet. Then I need ideas."

Cassie told her story, then answered questions, mostly dealing with the artifacts. Will Epps, their expert on Wormer texts and writing, after analyzing her scans, agreed that the artifacts were Wormer.

The team began reviewing and discarding proposals. Finally, Theodor made his decision. A platoon of marines would drop outside the Chadoran city. Three squads would act as a diversion, drawing warriors from the city, while one squad slipped in for a search and rescue. One hour later, a hopper would drop two mining subs at the berkelium site.

"Sir, the priestess dives there daily," Cassie said. "When they see our subs, they'll kill the team."

"That's why I'm giving the rescue squads an hour head start," Theodor replied. "It's not much, but our priority is to replenish our fuel before our orbit decays. I can't delay the berkelium extraction any longer."

Cassie slumped in her seat. *Davey, Liz*, she thought, *they're all going to die.*

Trask stood. "If Dr. Morant could provide a topographical display of the area, I'll outline the attack plan."

Cassie tapped some keys, and the planetary view of Griphus appeared, including the pattern of tectonic plates.

Like a jigsaw puzzle, Cassie thought. *Why can't this be that simple?*

"Zoom in to the landing site," Trask said.

Freezing the rotation over Pugnus and Manus, Cassie started to zoom in, then stopped, staring at the display. *No*, she thought, *it's too wild. But maybe...* She began tapping furiously, and calculations streamed across the holo.

"What the hell's going on?" Trask asked.

Theodor frowned. "Dr. Morant?"

Cassie looked at her results. *My god, it fits. But the time span...*

"Dr. Morant!" Theodor barked.

Cassie's head jerked up. Everyone was staring. *It's wild*, she thought, *but it fits.* And she liked things that fit.

"Captain," Cassie said, "what if we proved to the Chadorans that the deposit site is *not* sacred?"

Theodor frowned. "Discredit their religion? I don't—"

"No," Cassie said. "I mean, prove that it isn't sacred because..." She stopped. *What if she was wrong?* But it

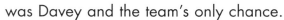

was Davey and the team's only chance.

"...because the third artifact isn't there," she finished.

Trask snorted. "Then why will they kill to protect the site?"

"Because they *think* it's there, based entirely on the diagrams on the artifacts."

"And you think those diagrams are wrong?" Theodor asked, but his voice held none of Trask's derision.

"I think they were correct once," she said. "But not any more."

"So where's the artifact?" Theodor asked.

Cassie's hand trembled as she tapped more keys. Two green lights appeared inland on the western coast of Manus, followed by a red light just off the same coast, forming the triangular pattern diagrammed on the artifacts.

"The two green lights are the known artifacts. The red light is both the supposed underwater location of the third and our targeted berkelium site."

She swallowed. *Here goes*, she thought.

"And this, I believe, is the actual location of the third artifact." A third green light appeared.

Everyone started talking at once. Theodor silenced them with a wave of his hand. He stared at the display.

On the eastern coast of Pugnus, on a separate continent and an entire ocean away from the underwater site, blinked the third green light.

Theodor turned to Cassie. "Explain."

"It involves tectonic plate theory—" she began.

"I know the theory. What's the relevance?"

Cassie tapped a key. The mid-oceanic trench between Pugnus and Manus glowed yellow.

"That trench is a 'divergent' boundary," Cassie said, "where new crust is being formed, pushing Manus and Pugnus further apart every year. But that also means that sometime in the past, they looked like this." The plates began to shift. The two large continents moved closer until the fist of Pugnus slipped into the open hand of Manus like a piece in a puzzle. Someone gasped, as the third green light on Pugnus aligned itself over the red light offshore of Manus.

Theodor nodded. "You're saying the Wormers originally placed the three artifacts as the diagrams show, but the missing one moved relative to the other two as the continents separated."

Xu shook his head. "Cassie..."

Cassie sighed. "I know. The time frame is...difficult to believe."

"How old are the artifacts if your theory is true?" Theodor asked.

Xu answered. "At least as old as the core sample from the deposit site, which formed as the trench started to spread. Cassie, what was the isotopic clock dating on the sample?"

Cassie hesitated. "Its age was thirty, uh..." She swallowed "...million years."

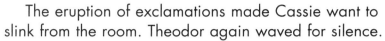

The eruption of exclamations made Cassie want to slink from the room. Theodor again waved for silence.

In desperation, Cassie turned to Will Epps. "We know that these ships are at least ten thousand years old. But couldn't they be much older?"

Several people squirmed. Their situation was bad enough without being reminded that they were relying on alien technology at least a hundred centuries old.

Will shrugged. "There's so much self-healing nano-tech, we can't estimate their age accurately."

"So any Wormer technology could be much older as well, right?" Cassie asked.

"But thirty million years..." Xu shook his head, as did others. She was losing them.

Cassie turned to Theodor.

"Captain, it all fits. It explains why the Chadorans have never found the artifact. Why our sub didn't see it. Why Wormers placed two artifacts on mountains, but supposedly put the third underwater. They didn't. They put it on land too."

"Can't we scan for the artifact?" Trask said.

"The other two don't show on scanners," Epps said. "They're shielded somehow."

"So the third artifact *could* be where the Chadorans say it is," Trask replied.

Cassie sat back, feeling defeated. Then something struck her.

"Both artifacts I saw are located over berkelium deposits, yet neither site appears on the mineral scans.

The artifacts shield the berkelium too."

"So?" Theodor said.

"We detected berkelium at the underwater site. That means nothing's shielding it. The third artifact isn't there."

Trask started to protest, but Theodor raised a hand. "I agree with Dr. Morant. It fits." He stood up. "Cassie, I'll give you the same lead time. Take a hopper down now."

Cassie was already sprinting for the door.

On a mountain plateau, across an ocean from where they had first landed on Griphus, Cassie and Davey stood, arms around each other's waist.

"So you saved me, the team, the entire ship," Davey said, "and made one of the most important discoveries in history. Not a bad day."

Cassie grinned. "Actually, the toughest part was convincing Cha-kay to fly in the hopper. Now she wants a world tour."

Beside them, happiness lighting her face, Cha-kay gazed at a huge glowing yellow sphere hovering above the ground.

The third artifact.

With one difference. A beam of energy shone from the sphere into the sky. The beam had begun the moment Cassie had touched the cube.

Cassie's per-comm beeped. It was Captain Theodor. "Dr. Morant, all three artifacts now appear on scanners,

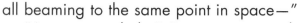

all beaming to the same point in space—"

"A new wormhole," Cassie interrupted.

Pause. "How'd you know?"

Cassie grinned. "Good guess."

"Hmm. Anyway, Earth's sending a second wormship. Good work. We'll all have the option of returning home or exploring the wormhole." Theodor signed off.

"You didn't mention your theory," Davey said.

"That the wormhole leads to the Wormers' home world? Just a hunch."

"Explain it to me then."

Cassie nodded at the cube. "I think the artifacts were a puzzle — and the wormhole the prize."

"For us or the Chadorans?"

"For us. Another bread crumb in the trail the Wormers left us." She shrugged and laughed. "It just fits."

Davey nodded. "So what about you? Back to Earth or through the wormhole?"

"Wormhole," she said.

He raised an eyebrow. "Okay, that surprised me."

Cassie grinned. "Hey, if the Wormers liked puzzles, they couldn't have been that bad." She stared at the artifact. "Besides, we solved their puzzle, saved ourselves, became heroes to the Chadorans..." Her eyes followed the beam up towards the heavens.

"Maybe we fit out here after all," she said softly.

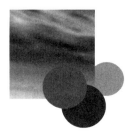

Skeeters

by MT O'Shaughnessy

Jack woke to find himself rolling from his sleeping couch. All he could do was blink and try to figure out where his arms and legs were. He had trouble deciding what was the edge of the couch and what was floor. Then, as the emergency lights flickered in his cabin, he forgot his awkward position and tried to focus on what had happened. *Was happening.*

It was quiet – too quiet. It felt just like it did after a loud storm, the kind of silence that said something even worse might be around the corner. Then a sharp pain in his left shin brought him back, informing him where the couch strap had gone. Around him the lights steadied and the almost undetectable motion of the ship stopped. He hadn't noticed the gentle swaying until it was gone.

"Mom! Dad!"

His voice echoed flatly. He heard nothing, not even the auto-response of the ship's artificial intelligence, Eos. He should have.

Jack struggled to untangle himself from the couch's grip of blankets, sheets, and strap.

He hurried to the door.

The door whined at him. He had to shoulder his way through the widening gap, forcing it open. Around him the light brightened from emergency to standard day, making him realize how dim it had been before.

He wanted to run to the Control Room and find his parents, but ship habits made him stop and turn back to gather the loose equipment and make sure it was secure. Jack knew that anything left untethered was an even worse accident waiting to happen. If the grav-gens went offline, anything loose would become a free-floating hazard.

What was the greatest hazard in space? Jack tried to keep calm as he realized he'd opened his door without checking the hall for air or putting on his suit.

No taking chances. He pulled out his personal emergency suit. The training sessions with his parents paid off. Jack counted out the steps under his breath, as calmly as if this was another drill.

He finished by shoving on the helmet and then running a finger down the quickseal at the front of the suit. He went through the checklist in his head, trying to be certain he knew what he needed to do next.

Once again Jack called for his parents. His hope that

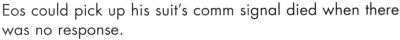

Eos could pick up his suit's comm signal died when there was no response.

As he walked down the corridor, Jack watched for any more unsecured equipment. He didn't like the way the lights still flickered from time to time. At least it felt as though the grav-gens were working. He considered seeing if his workstation in the Medlab was active. Maybe he should check in there first.

No, Jack told himself, the ship protocol was to get to Control as quickly as possible and assess the situation. He didn't have time to think about anything else. He had to join his parents and find out what had happened

Hoping he wasn't forgetting something, he did just that.

As he entered the Control Room, Jack could hear the voice of Eos, the ship's AI, through his helmet.

"Mr. Field, I am afraid other than visuals, most exterior sensors are offline. Interior sensors are functioning at fifty percent efficiency and I cannot accurately assess the entire damage done to the ship. Functionality of the navigation and outside communication systems are unknown. It appears exterior communications are working, however I cannot verify that I am indeed broadcasting. In-ship comms are not functioning, as is evidenced by the lack of contact from Jack —"

Jack pulled off his helmet and interrupted. "Dad! Mom! I'm here. Hey Eos… you okay?"

"I continue to function, Jack. How well we are determining. Thank you for asking."

Jack's mother, Helen Field, gathered Jack in a quick hug. He tried not to squirm immediately out of her grasp. It might be comforting, but he still had his duties.

"Jack appears to be physically undamaged. Sensors in Control are fully operational and I can detect no injuries."

Sighing in relief, Helen gave him an extra little squeeze.

"What happened? My room was all messed up." Jack asked his father over his mother's shoulder. "I cleaned up what I could. There was air," he finally thought to add, a little embarrassed he hadn't reported this first.

"Looks like we crashed. We still don't know why, or where. Are you sure you're okay, Jack?" Steven Field asked.

"I'm fine. How's the ship?" Steven wasn't only Jack's father. He was the pilot and captain of their family ship, the *Silslip*. As a cargo ship, *Silslip* had one of the better reputations in the star lanes. She'd certainly never crashed before, Jack thought worriedly. Both of Jack's parents' helmets gleamed on the floor at Steven's feet. Their gray emergency suits were opened at the neck but otherwise sealed.

"We're checking now." His parents returned their attention to the screens.

Jack moved around his mother and toward a free

workstation. He quickly called up data on the three medical rooms that formed the Medlab. It was his job to be sure the equipment in those rooms functioned and that the stockroom was full. It looked like the scanner room was a bit damaged, but the other two appeared to have survived the crash in working order. Jack frowned to himself. There was something else he should check, but what?

His thoughts were interrupted when Steven asked Eos about their surroundings. Jack listened.

"As I said, Mr. Fields, I lack any precision in my readings."

Helen asked, "Do we know where we are, Eos?"

"Not yet, Mrs. Field. However I do detect intermittent broadcasts from this planet to an unknown offworld location. Given time I may be able to intercept sufficient broadcasts to clarify our position. All I can verify is that there is a Tierian communication beacon on this planet."

"Which is a good thing, right, Dad?" Jack asked in the following silence.

For a moment Steven frowned, then slowly nodded.

"Y-e-s… Yes, it is. Even if it's only automated, we should be able to fix it so we can transmit a rescue call. Yes, it's a good thing."

Helen looked thoughtful as she said: "First we need to figure out if we can get to the beacon or not. We need to know what's outside."

Jack knew his mother had studied xenoplanetology, so of course the conditions on the planet were never far from her mind. She often teased him and his father that without her they'd forget to check if the air outside the 'locks was breathable, let alone if a human might be comfortable there. His mother was right. They needed to learn more about where they'd landed.

Jack touched the small pad at the entrance to the Medlab and waited as the light in the enclosure slowly grew to normal levels. Thankfully it looked as though its systems still worked.

As his parents had worked on Eos' external sensors, Jack had realized why he kept worrying about forgetting something. He had.

He went straight to the table at the far wall, empty except for a rectangular case fastened to the top, containing drifts of sand. From inside it came a soft whispering sound. A flowing form of crystal moved to the glass, legs clicking against the window. Smiling, Jack tapped back.

The inhabitant of the case came from Palick's World, the *Silslip's* last stop. Palick's World was the largest known source of natural glass as well as several important silicates. And was the only planet known to have silicon-silicate lifeforms. Like Spinky.

Jack had taken an instant liking to the little creature. When they were motionless the Spines, as most people called them, looked like spiders crossed with millipedes. Their entire bodies were made of what looked like foggy

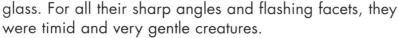

glass. For all their sharp angles and flashing facets, they were timid and very gentle creatures.

Jack had found Spinky hiding in their cargo bay when they left Palick's World. His mother had helped him figure out how to care for the harmless, friendly creature.

Jack tapped a button and held out his hand as the window of the case slid away. Spinky clinked and slithered onto his hand. About the size of a small cat, Spinky weighed next to nothing. His pointed legs scuttled as he climbed Jack's arm and rested on his shoulder.

Jack took one last look around the Medlab, closing down the enclosure's power. Other than a few smaller pieces of equipment spilled onto the floor, the main room had been undamaged by the crash.

Heading back to Control, Jack guessed he'd wasted enough time. With him out from underfoot, his parents should have figured out where they were.

He took a small power cell from his pocket and handed it up to Spinky. Jack had found the Spine liked to play with them. It seemed to keep him calm, and the gentle rocking motion of the Spine rolling the power cell between its forelegs was soothing against Jack's shoulders.

Jack paused as a reflection caught his eye. Down a side corridor, under a closed port, a small glittering patch looked out of place.

Careful not to touch the silver liquid, Jack checked the port. It was closed. It appeared the interior seal had broken in the landing, but the exterior safety shield had been activated. Whatever it was must have spilled in the time it had taken for the port to reseal.

His parents needed to know about this, he decided.

Helen straightened up from her crouch with a frown. She studied the small device in her hand and tapped a few glowing lights on its screen.

Her voice was distracted as she said, "Looks like almost pure mercury... Steven, hand me the...thanks."

Jack noticed his parents did that a lot. They ended each other's sentences and tended to know what the other wanted just before anything was said.

Steven handed over another scanning device and kept silent. Perched on Jack's shoulder, Spinky seemed content to roll the cell between six forelegs with a faint tapping sound.

Helen finally nodded and looked up from the spill. "It definitely is mercury. I think I remember something... I can't place it..." she said. "We should head back to Control and ask Eos."

When they entered Control, Helen called Eos up immediately. "Eos? I vaguely remember something about a solar system with a large amount of mercury on one of its planets... do we have any files on it?"

For a long second there was silence. Then Eos spoke quietly on the room's speakers. "Yes. I have a record of a few news service files and a single navigational plot point. Melthazar. Second planet of the system, it is comparable to Earth in size and density. It has a similar atmosphere, although I would not suggest breathing it for extended periods. No known lifeforms of lower or higher class. It houses a single Tierian outpost for limited scientific study of the one notable aspect of the system."

"Mercury oceans," Helen said with satisfaction. "Now, I remember."

"Yes, Mrs. Field. Apparently there are a series of naturally formed bodies of liquid mercury on Melthazar that for sake of convention are called 'oceans.' Using the data on this world on file, the location of the science station beacon, which I have now ascertained as being on far side of the nearest continent, and my line of sight readings, I calculate we are approximately 1.5 kilometers from land."

A faintly distorted image came up on the screen. A level plain of silvery gray stretched out as far as the horizon. Frowning, Jack's dad nodded and muttered, "Knowing what I'm looking at, I can see it's liquid mercury ... otherwise I would have thought the video pickups were messed up."

Helen looked relieved and smiled at Jack, kissing his head in a quick swoop downward. Steven, however, looked distracted.

"Eos, how deep is this ocean?" Steven asked.

"According to data, a rough estimate for this area is close to one kilometer deep."

Making a small noise in the back of his throat, Steven nodded to himself.

35

"But the ship will keep floating until we're rescued — won't it, Eos?" Jack asked, frightened by the sight of all that poisonous mercury.

"One moment."

There was a pause as the family looked at one another.

"Jack. I am sorry to say, no. We are not capable of prolonged flotation. There is too much damage to our hull. The ship is filling up with mercury."

Eos had been able to make contact with the Tierian science outpost. The scientists were aware they had crashed and had already sent out a rescue team. It would take three hours to reach the *Silslip*. They had time to pack, but they wouldn't be able to save everything.

Back in the cargo bay, Jack helped his mother load a portable datablock, keying in the commands to transfer files from one of her many notebooks. Next to him, the large glittering blocks of natural glass that were this trip's cargo, tinkled and chimed as Spinky raced over their surfaces. At least some one was happy, Jack thought.

His father certainly wasn't. It looked like the whole shipment was going to be lost. And most of Helen's experiments and research would have to be left behind.

Jack's stuff was easier to handle. He only had a few notes from his school journals and some bits of clothing. He'd not really had a chance to collect a lot yet, so he

didn't think he was going to miss much. Definitely not some of the teaching programs.

Jack heard a splash. Both he and his mother turned to look down the long rows of glass blocks.

Where the stacks of glass cubes met the darker cubes of the silicates and rare silicons, Jack could just make out a silvery sheen. And a moving form.

"Spinky!"

Dropping the notebook, Jack ran down the aisle. Helen carefully put down the datablock and followed.

In the deeper shadows, Jack found Spinky spinning on the surface of a large pool of mercury. He had to laugh. "Mom! He's playing... I thought he was in trouble... he's having fun. Look at him!"

Helen smiled as she watched before asking, "I wonder if it could have any adverse effects on him though... as a silicon life form I don't know how he'd react to it..." She hunted for the source of the mercury, then gasped.

Looking around to find out what was wrong, he found her staring at a large hole that softly burbled with incoming silver liquid.

"We've got a major leak."

Plugging his personal sensor device into a port, with its scan of the leak, Steven waited while Eos recalculated. Jack could tell his father was worried by the way he took his mother's hand. Jack was trying to act like nothing

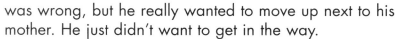

was wrong, but he really wanted to move up next to his mother. He just didn't want to get in the way.

After a moment Eos finished.

"Mr. and Mrs. Fields, I suggest we begin to plan for an immediate evacuation. The ship will submerge completely before the Tierian team arrives."

Eos' soft murmur somehow made the words that much more frightening. Jack gave in and shuffled forward to duck under his mother's arm. His father looked down and smiled slightly at Jack. Reaching out, he put his hand on Jack's head. "It'll be okay. Promise," he said.

Jack nodded, not sure what to say. He knew what it meant if they couldn't get off the *Silslip* before the Tierians arrived. He just wished he didn't feel so helpless. Everything seemed to happen over his head, between his parents and Eos.

Suddenly he realized the Spinky wasn't with him. Jack squirmed out of his parents' arms. "I'll be right back," he said over his shoulder as he left. "Spinky is still in the cargo bay."

Jack shivered as he ran down the corridor. Somehow the normally pleasant soft light and pale shadows had become claustrophobic. Jack tried to throw off the impression. All he really wanted was some one who needed his help, some one he *could* help, and Spinky was it.

Once back at the bay he slowed down. The cargo bay had always bothered Jack, but he'd never figured out why. Now he had more than enough reason and it was slowly filling the aisle.

There was Spinky, still skittering and twirling on the mercury. For a moment Jack decided he could just forget the rest of it and enjoy Spinky's antics. He looked like a giant skeeter made of glass, skimming across the surface of the mercury like it was a steady floor.

Jack's parents joined him in the cargo bay. His mother looked red around the eyes and his father wasn't much better, always a sure sign that he was worried. Jack figured they'd decided something but he didn't think they were going to tell him.

They had walked in to find him sitting close to the growing pool. He'd been laughing as he watched Spinky do more and more complicated maneuvers across the small pond.

Together the three of them watched Spinky in silence.

The moment dragged on and on, worrying Jack. Surely something could be done, they weren't going to just sit there and... what? They didn't have a lot of time, did they? So what were they doing standing there, saying nothing?

Suddenly, Jack was afraid he understood, too well. Rather than face the moment, or be brave, or keep listening to the awful silence, Jack pointed at Spinky.

"Look, Dad. He can skate like those bugs at home! But on the mercury. I think he really likes it. Mom? Do the Spines have lakes and stuff on Palick's World?

40

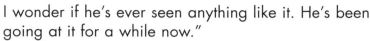

I wonder if he's ever seen anything like it. He's been going at it for a while now."

When neither of his parents said anything, his voice dropped. "It looks like fun. If only we could do it…"

Jack was about to continue saying something, anything, not wanting the inevitable to come crashing down on him. But his father's sudden gasp and the unconsciously hard clench of his fingers on Jack's shoulder stopped him.

Helen worriedly asked, "What? Steven? What?!"

"Follow me!" his father shouted.

Scrambling, Jack got to his feet and started to follow after his already running parents. He stopped to grab the slightly confused looking Spinky. The creature had no more idea what was going on with all the noise and motion than Jack did.

"It can work, Mr. Fields. It is a very interesting concept."

Eos' affirmation of the plan visibly relaxed Jack's parents. Without knowing why, Jack relaxed as well. He wasn't sure he understood half of what they'd been talking about on the way to Control.

Steven began to give orders. "Jack, get Spinky to the Medlab scanners. Helen, we're going to need weights and some calculations for each of us. I'll get the fabricators working. We'll meet in the main bay in fifteen minutes.

We've got that long to get everything together. It's going to take Eos a good five more minutes after that until he's done the designs. Then we'll need at least six minutes per boot, meaning just under an hour. And that's when things are going to get tight." He nodded confidently. "So go! Go! Eos, start the designs!"

"I have already, Mr. Field. Estimated time of completion: forty six point three minutes."

Jack was already racing down the corridor toward the cargo bay. He could hear his mother behind him asking questions of Eos' medical and math sections as his father clomped along the corridor behind him, catching up quickly.

Steven and Jack reached the cross corridor to the Medlab at the same time. Steven halted a moment, looking at Jack. Jack had no idea what the look on his father's face meant, but he didn't have time to think about it. It was clear that whatever was going on, he had to get to the scanners. Behind him, Jack heard his father hurrying past to the cargo bay and its fabricators.

Spinky rode the rise and fall of Jack's shoulder as steadily as if he was standing still. Jack was glad Spinky seemed to be calm. It was going to make things easier. Not that either of them knew what was going on.

As he came to the door it was already sliding open. Eos' voice sounded from inside.

"Hello Jack. I have prepared the equipment in anticipation of your arrival. I would request you utilize the table that is illuminated."

A single black table in the center of the room was spot lit. A few of the monitors and screens around the room flickered to life, a smaller number remained completely blank. This room was showing signs of the crash where the main room hadn't. Luckily the scanners were still functioning.

"Standard scan or is there something more specific needed, Eos?" Jack asked.

"Jack, we will need to use a sub cellular scan. We need a clear view of the structure of the creature's legs, and a sub cellular scan should accomplish this although the physiology is different."

Carefully placing Spinky on the table, murmuring to him, Jack made sure to keep Spinky still. Thinking about it a moment he stopped part way through the process.

"Eos? Wouldn't it be better to do a multiple scan to get a look at all the legs? Couldn't there be a slight difference among them, according to use? I think I remember one of my biology courses saying something like that..."

"Very good, Jack, I had not considered this. I am rather busy at the moment. Proceed please."

At Jack's command a light grew from within the gleaming black surface, a wave of green that rippled underneath Spinky. It was over in an instant. Patting Spinky, Jack carefully placed him back on his shoulder. Spinky made a small sound, almost as if he were amused by the whole procedure.

Jack walked up to the nearest wall screen and watched as the scan of Spinky appeared. Slowly it rotated and grew, enlarging one of his legs. A second image appeared next to it, a secondary leg. For a moment several others flashed across the screen and Jack saw there were indeed small differences between them. But the images got bigger and bigger, focusing on the tips of each. Here they were identical.

Jack could hear his mother and Eos discussing it over the network.

"Mrs. Field, it is as I suspected. If you look at the level that would be analogous of 'cellular' in a human, you will see the small blades on the Spine's legs. The specific flexible curve of the Spine leg is capable of distributing its weight on the plane of the mercury sufficiently to remain above the surface."

And Jack could see what they were talking about.

The leg was curved outward slightly at its tip. And the surface looked like it was scaly, small discs growing from its side. They reminded Jack of a fungus he had seen on a tree on Earth, once. But these were incredibly small and seemed to cup downward.

Jack was beginning to see what they were thinking.

Spinky could spread his weight out and move across the mercury because of the specific curve of the tips of his legs as well as the small scales or cups. Each formed an extra bit of surface that helped keep him on top of the mercury, rather than sinking.

"Eos, I see it. Can you make something to do the same job? I just don't know enough about the weight distribution to be sure, myself," Helen said.

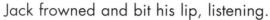

Jack frowned and bit his lip, listening.

"Mrs. Fields, I can design something that should utilize the same principles if not identical materials. The cargo we have aboard are more than sufficient. And with several datablocks I have on the subject, the preliminary surface structure is completed. With your calculations on each of the crew's individual weight and height, I can finish with the final structure's shape."

Jack didn't understand completely the math and science of what they were talking about. But he did suddenly see what his father had meant. With Eos' help they were going to build boots of some kind out of the cargo glass.

Since he was there, his job done, and a science station looked active, Jack went over to tap in some commands. Muting his mother's and Eos' conversation, he called up information on mercury and its properties.

After a little bit of reading, he finally understood. Mercury didn't stick to glass. Or rather mercury stuck to itself with more strength than it could stick to glass.

Using this, and the way Spinky's legs were made, they were going to make a set of 'boots' that wouldn't stick to mercury and would let them walk on its surface. Hopefully.

Jack shut down the console as his father called him down to the bay.

Jack carefully pulled the first set of boots on to his feet while his mother muttered and paced behind him. Steven was leaning close and talking quietly.

"Ok, now, Jack, be careful. Despite making this as strong as we could, we don't know exactly how the boots will hold up. And we do *not* have time to make a second set for anybody. So take it slow and easy."

Turning from the fabricator on another one of her passes, Helen moved close.

"I don't like it," she said.

"I know, but he's the lightest. If we can't get the design to work for the lightest, what chance..." his father's voice trailed off.

Behind them the fabricator chimed once. Another boot was done. Larger, it was for one of Jack's parents, and it slowly slid into the light.

Jack frowned in concentration while working at not falling over. It had taken him a bit to stand up, each second waiting for the sound of shattering glass. As it was, he felt strange being supported slightly above the floor by a mass of glass strands.

Those strands spread from his knees and lower leg out into a wide circle of glittering material. The pad they made flexed and moved, spreading as he put his foot down and contracting around his leg as he lifted the other. The shape from above, when spread out, was an oval that looked almost like an egg. Jack's mother had said it was so all his weight was spread out as evenly as possible.

When he moved the boots sang like a chime. Concentrating, and moving slowly, Jack walked toward the growing pool in the aisle of the bay. At the edge he stopped, the clashing and chiming of the glass softening to silence.

All of them held their breath as he slowly stepped onto the surface of the mercury.

Spinky rushed down his arm, jumping onto the liquid. Jack almost fell as he started in surprise.

He had no idea how to use the boots, nor did his parents. Jack wondered how they were going to get off the ship. But they did have an expert on board, he thought, and watched, really watched, how Spinky moved.

Spinky never had less than four of his ten feet touching the liquid at once. He had a rolling walk, making it look like he almost rippled.

Frowning, Jack slid one foot forward.

Immediately part of the boot submerged in the glittering liquid and Steven yelled out. Almost overbalancing again, Jack looked over his shoulder.

Smiling to assure his parents that everything was fine, not really believing it himself, he slide forward his other foot.

Still slightly submerged, this one steadied and held. Carefully he moved forward, step by slow step. When he reached the center of the pool he knew for sure it could work for him. And he was starting to get the hang of it.

Behind him his father grunted.

"Huh. I didn't think of that. We can't just 'step.' We need to slide as well. Very good, Jack!"

Smiling to himself, Jack turned slowly and carefully.

"Once you get going, it's really very easy. Honest, Mom, it's like the time you took me cross country skiing," he said as he returned to his parents.

No one mentioned the fact that while it had worked for Jack, no one knew if it would work for his parents.

It wasn't too surprising to find the surface of Melthazar's ocean incredibly bright. Even with his helmet dimmed, Jack still had the urge to squint.

Beside him, his parents carefully balanced on their own sets of boots at the edge of the ship. Compared to Jack, they were a bit awkward and he could see his mother was really nervous. For a change he was giving them lessons. He moved ahead and circled slowly so he could face them.

No one talked about the fact that while they had walked down the corridors in the ship, his parents had yet to see if their boots would work on the mercury.

Behind them, the *Silslip* was more than half sub-merged now. They had had to use one of the top 'locks. It was wide open, and only a few feet from the strange ocean's surface. What little they could carry with them was already in packs, Jack's feeling light right now. He

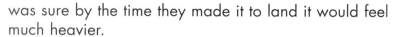

was sure by the time they made it to land it would feel much heavier.

At Jack's feet, for all the world looking like he'd just found Heaven, Spinky was happily circling and spinning around his boots. Smiling, trying to ignore the fact that their home was sinking, Jack turned and looked at his parents.

"Eos, you still online?" he asked the large datablock his father carried.

"Yes, Jack. Thank you."

Eos' voice came over the suit's comm system. It was as calm and quiet as usual. Jack wondered if the AI would miss the *Silslip* too.

Ignoring all of his internal questions, Jack took a deep breath and began.

"Ok, then. We're set to go? Mom, Dad? Ok, first try to think of it as skiing or skating..."

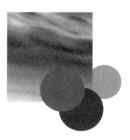

Tides of Change

by Sarah Jane Elliott

"Absolutely not!"

Zac glowered at his mother. "But all the kids are wearing it like this!"

"If all the kids decided to jump out an airlock, would you do it too?" She planted her hands firmly on his shoulders and pushed him toward his room. "I have a very important conference this evening, and I'm not going to spend it explaining why my son looks like a nickel-plated porcupine. You get back to your room and sonic that stuff out of your hair."

51

Zac stomped back to his room and stood in front of his mirror. His mother, he concluded, was crazy. The chrome spikes sticking out from his head looked fracking cool — but moms never understood these things. He sighed, picked up the styler, and set about pulling the alloy from his hair.

"Being the son of the Governor," he said quietly, "sucks."

She'd never been this bad on Earth. Oh, she'd been a Mom, but she'd been kinda cool sometimes. And he'd been able to get away from her every other weekend to go visit Dad. But then she'd gotten the job as Governor of Oceanus Colony on Altaris, and before Zac even knew what was happening, she'd packed up all their things and shuttled them off to this fracking planet at the back end of the galaxy.

"The tides of change are turning." His mom said stuff like that. *"Think about it, Zac. We'll be part of the mission to prove that a civilian colony can actually work. We'll be making history."*

"History," Zac said, "sucks."

Back home, he'd never had to worry about looking good for the colony reporters. Back home, he'd had friends. But here, all anyone saw was the goody-goody squit he had to be for his mom.

Back home, he'd never had to worry about things like whether or not Callie Williams would have laughed at him if he'd asked her to the Conjunction Dance.

He'd tried talking to his mom about it, but she didn't

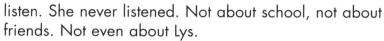

listen. She never listened. Not about school, not about friends. Not even about Lys.

He keyed up the display on his wrist-comp, and read over the five-year-old colony archive entry he had found.

Oceanographer Vanishes with Young Daughter

ALTARIS — Fatma Khatri, renowned oceanographer and a founding member of Oceanus Colony, vanished yesterday during a routine survey of Connor's Reef. With Khatri was her daughter, Lysithea, age eight. Rescue crews continue to search the area ...

Zac shut down the display and returned his attention to his hair. It *had* to be Lys. Lysithea. He wrinkled his nose. The stupid Jupiter names may have died out pretty fast, but they'd been really popular with parents in the year after the Zeus Station disaster. Sometimes he was thankful that his mother had a thing for classical authors.

"Isaac," his mother said, sticking her head in the door.

Sometimes he wasn't. "Don't call me that, Mom."

She ignored him, as usual. "I don't want you staying out any later than twenty-six."

"But the conjunction isn't 'till twenty-four and a half!"

"Which will give you plenty of time to get home after you see it."

Zac raked his hands through his hair as his mother left the room. On second thought, he was glad she never listened. She'd probably throw a fit if she ever found out about Lys.

He lowered his hands and ran his finger down the long barb embedded beneath the skin of his forearm. He remembered Lys's words after she had pulled him from the water, hurt and terrified, broken shards of coral still embedded in his hands and feet. She had glanced in disgust at the remains of his waverunner, and then placed her hand over the barb, splaying her fingers so that the webbing between them showed clearly.

"Is Her punishment and promise," Lys had said, in her hesitant, accented Commonwealth. *"If She wants, if She needs, She change you as She changed me."*

Zac looked at his reflection and smiled. That boy in the mirror, who nobody liked, with the stupid brown hair that wouldn't stay out of his eyes now that it wasn't sticking up in spikes anymore, was the only colonist on Altaris who knew the secret of Connor's Reef.

Still grinning, Zac got up to change for the dance.

Asimov, the larger moon, peeked above the horizon, but the smaller Heinlein hadn't risen yet. When he had

first come to Altaris, they'd still been called AS-1 and AS-2. Zac sighed. They never should have let his mother name the moons.

Callie stood on the edge of the dance square, talking to Ananke Singh and Leda Krantz. The flashing lights strung around the field turned Callie's hair into a golden halo around her head. Zac clenched his fists. He was going to do it. Girls had gone out with him back on Earth, why wouldn't Callie?

She looked up as he approached, her blue eyes made darker and deeper by the moonlight.

"Hey, Callie?"

"Yes?" she said.

"Would you like to dance?"

Callie's burst of laughter struck Zac like a slap. "With you?" Behind her, Leda and Ananke were helpless with giggles. Callie could barely keep hers under control as she said, "Um, not really, no."

His cheeks burning, Zac began to back away from the trio of hysterical girls, but something blocked his way. Turning, he found himself staring up at Gan Fielding.

Gan looked over Zac's head. "He bugging you, Callie?"

"No," Callie laughed. "I haven't had this much fun all night!"

Gan snickered and shoved Zac, sending him sprawling across the grass. "Callie is so out of your league, squit. Go try the primary kids."

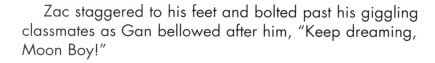

Zac staggered to his feet and bolted past his giggling classmates as Gan bellowed after him, "Keep dreaming, Moon Boy!"

Zac ran. Away from the school, away from the students, away from the laughter that followed him long after he shouldn't have been able to hear it anymore. He hit the forest and kept running, his feet pounding the ground as he ran blindly through the trees. And then, suddenly, he was standing in bright moonlight, and he skidded to a stop.

He looked around in surprise. He'd run all the way to the Khalimbe estuary — the deep, narrow corridor where the Khalimbe River emptied out into Connor's Bay. He couldn't help but feel a little impressed with himself.

The water was low in the ravine, which the river had carved from the bedrock over thousands of years. Zac began to pick his way down the rocks toward the water's edge. When the rock beneath his fingers became rougher about halfway down, he grinned, remembering his last geology exam. "Thanocene Era." The hundreds of fossils embedded in that layer of rock made for some great handholds.

His feet hit seaweed when he was still about a dozen meters from the water, and his descent became easier — the seaweed anchored itself firmly to the rocks, and as long as he was careful where he stepped in the slippery mess, he could get a good hold. A few of the bladders in the leaves popped beneath his hand.

57

Zac took a closer look at the seaweed. Mr. Li had told them that the bladders got bigger as the seaweed got deeper, because they needed more air to lift them through the water. They'd been getting bigger for a while as Zac descended, but now they were getting smaller again as he moved deeper into the ravine. He wondered if Mr. Li would let him do his science exhibition on it; the teacher was notoriously picky about what he considered a suitable project. "At least I might get something good out of this fracking night," Zac muttered.

He finally reached the water, and busied himself for a while by lifting the seaweed with his feet and watching the crustaceans he uncovered go scuttling off to hide. He breathed deep of the salty, weedy smell of the ocean. It was nice here, away from the noise and chatter of the dance. All he could hear now was the singsong burbling of the water rushing over the river stones. He looked up at the sky, which was brighter now that Heinlein's light was beginning to glow on the horizon, and sighed.

And then there was nothing but silence.

His eyes snapped open. The water had stopped flowing completely, and sat like a thin coating of glass over the stones at the bottom of the estuary.

A flash caught his eye, and Zac gasped. On a rock in the middle of the water, the moonslight glittered off the carapace of a rock jewel.

Rock jewels resembled Earth crabs, and were normally dull brown and boring to look at. But when the animal inside the shell abandoned it for a new home, the shell became black and iridescent, sparkling like some dark gem. The legs stayed attached to the shell, and though they normally clutched tight to whatever surface the rock jewel had left them on, they could be made to open and close by pressing the spot where they joined the shell. Rock jewel hair clips were the rage with the girls, but because empty rock jewel shells were so rare, nobody in his class had a real one.

Until now.

He stepped carefully along some of the bigger rocks that poked out of the water, not wanting to get his shoes wet. He slipped a few times on the slick carpet of seaweed that covered the rocks, but finally made it to the one bearing his prize.

The soft music of water startled him, and he looked up to see that the water had started to flow again — but it wasn't flowing out toward the Bay anymore. It was flowing in from it.

Zac shrugged and bent to retrieve the rock jewel, but getting the legs to release the seaweed was trickier than he had expected. He distracted himself by imagining the look on Callie's face when he gave it to her. She'd look at him in surprise, and then smile as she realized that she'd been wrong about him. Zac couldn't wait to see Gan's expression when Callie went with *him* to the next dance. He tugged harder at the stubborn shell, but it took him another ten minutes before the glittering carapace finally came free. Zac stood, his arms raised in a triumphant pose, and froze.

Way out in the Bay, the top of Connor's Reef stuck up from the water like a row of jagged teeth.

Zac's heart began to beat faster. He'd never seen the Reef exposed before, not even at low tide. He turned to make his way back to the bank, and saw that his stepping stones were gone. The babbling of the water was louder now as it flowed past the rock on which he stood. As Zac watched, the water crept up over the edge of the rock and lapped at his shoes.

He lifted a foot quickly out of the water. "Great, now I'm gonna have salt stains."

Zac locked the legs of the rock jewel to the hem of his shirt and peered into the water at his feet. He could barely make out the rocks in the moonlight, but the water covering them didn't look that deep. He stretched out his foot and stepped to the first rock, teetered for a moment, and caught his balance.

"That wasn't so bad." He felt around in the water for the next one. The river rushed around his ankles now — it was definitely moving faster. Trying to convince his heart to stop beating so loud, he found the next stone. He was straddling the water between them when the river picked up speed and tugged at his feet. He might have been all right on plain wet rocks, but the ones he was standing on were covered in slippery seaweed. With a yelp, he splashed down into the river.

He gasped as cold water immediately soaked him to the knees. "*Frack!*" He cringed as his voice echoed off the rock walls of the estuary, and glanced sheepishly

over his shoulder. Then he tried to step up to the next
stone.

He couldn't move his right foot. He yanked hard, but
it wouldn't budge. Catching his lip between his teeth, he
bent down and ran his hands along his leg until he dis-
covered the problem. His foot was wedged firmly
between two of the stones hidden beneath the surface of
the water.

The river had reached his waist, and it was running
so fast that he was having trouble keeping his balance.
He pulled at his foot and at the rocks, but it was no
good. Zac staggered as the current swept his free foot
out from under him, and got a mouthful of brackish
water before he managed to stand up again.

Trying hard not to cry, he fumbled at his wrist-comp
and keyed in his mother's emergency code.

"Governor Jones." His mom sounded busy and irritated.

"Mom!"

"Oh, Isaac, really, I've told you not to use this code
unless it's an em—"

He splashed again and got another mouthful of
water. "Mom, help me!"

"Isaac?" She didn't sound irritated anymore. She
sounded scared. "Zac, where are you?"

"I'm in—" The current pushed him down again, and
by the time he'd struggled back up, his wrist-comp had
shorted out.

Water pounded against his chest, roaring like thunder
as it rushed into the estuary. Sobbing openly now, not

caring how it made him look, Zac jerked desperately at his foot. On the last tug, his good foot slipped again and he went back under the water. But no matter how hard he struggled, the water was moving too fast, pinning him down. He couldn't get back to the surface.

Pain like a needle of fire stabbed in his arm and began to spread through his veins. His muscles stopped responding to his frantic thrashing signals, his lungs stopped aching for air, his heart stopped pounding.

For an instant, all he was aware of was that burning heat coursing through his body, and then everything went black.

Zac felt the crunch as his waverunner hit the reef, and then he was flying though the air. He stared dumbly down as the water rushed up to meet him.

He landed hard, branches of coral slicing through his skin as his fall shattered the lacy, delicate structures. The water closed over his head. Trying not to cry out, he opened his eyes, and watched in horror as a thin, dark tendril emerged from a broken stump of coral and wrapped around his wrist. Then he did scream as the tendril stabbed into his forearm, leaving a long black barb embedded beneath the skin. He began to choke. He couldn't breathe. He was going to drown.

The next thing he knew, he was lying on solid ground, and someone was shaking him. He coughed, spitting up water, and stared at the girl holding him.

Her eyes were so dark that he couldn't tell where the pupil stopped and the iris began. The sun had darkened her skin to a rich brown and bleached streaks into her tangled black hair. She wore a tattered pair of shorts that were a little too small, and an equally ragged Mars University shirt that was a little too big.

She was also soaking wet.

"Who—" Zac began.

"You hurt Her." The girl's face was flushed with anger.

"Who?" Zac asked.

She gestured sharply toward the shards of coral floating in the water. "Her!"

Zac frowned. "The reef?" He tried to sit up, and the pain in his arm made his head reel. He hissed and grabbed at it when he saw the barb beneath his skin.

The girl gave him a rueful smile and held up her own arm. Her hand was webbed all the way up to the first knuckle on each finger. And she had a barb identical to his beneath her skin.

"Is Her punishment and promise," she said. "If She wants, if She needs, She change you as She changed me."

"Change into what?"

The girl's grin widened, showing her teeth. "Into Her guardian."

He stared out at the water. "You mean...the reef is alive?"

She looked at him in disgust. "All reefs, on all planets, are alive. This Reef is smart. She thinks. She feels." She looked out over the water. "She hurts."

"I'm sorry," said Zac. "It was an accident."

"I know," she said. "She knows. So you live."

"But this change—" he protested. "It's not fair! I have a life, you know."

"It took Her centuries to grow as big as She was, and you destroy so much of Her in a day." She plucked a coral shard from the beach. "This part of Her dies. Those creatures She sheltered and gave nourishment to die. Is your life more important than theirs?" She looked as if she was about to say more, but she stiffened suddenly, looking out over the water. After another moment, Zac heard it too, and swore softly. Engines. His waverunner would have sent out a distress beacon when it hit the reef.

The girl got to her feet and ran. Zac tried to follow, but his head swam and the world tilted, and he found himself sprawled across the sand again. "Wait!"

She paused, already up to her waist in the ocean.

"I'm Zac," he said.

She stared at him for a moment, and smiled. "I am— "

Zac's lungs heaved, spewing water across the rock beneath him. Moaning, he rolled over and found himself staring up into angry dark eyes. "Lys!"

He tried to sit up, but a webbed hand planted firmly on his chest kept him down. "Are you stupid?" she demanded.

He looked around, trying to figure out what had happened. He was lying at the edge of the forest. His shoe was gone, but his foot seemed fine. It didn't even hurt that much.

But his arm was throbbing.

"What happened?"

"You were drowning," Lys said quietly. "She heard. Called me. I came, but not fast enough. So She changed you."

Zac felt a wave of cold creep up his spine as he looked down at the barb in his arm. "The burning?"

Lys nodded. "Her venom."

"Can She stop it?"

"No." Lys looked down at her own arm. "Not once change starts. Was the only way to save you." Her mood shifted abruptly, and she smacked him lightly on the side of his head. "Why were you down there? Did you not see the tide coming in?"

"Er, yeah," he said. "But I've watched the tide come in before. I didn't think it'd come that fast."

Lys made a noise of complete disgust. "*Trees* are smarter than you!"

He looked at where she pointed. The river, high in the estuary, stretched between them and the opposite shore. He cringed. The trees stopped just as the water began. If he'd been paying closer attention, he would have noticed that all the vegetation ended there in a fairly straight line. "Yeah, but—"

She waved something under his nose. It was a piece of seaweed. "And did you not see balloons getting smaller?"

"Yeah," said Zac, "but our teacher said they were smaller in *shallower* water."

"And in *faster*," Lys said. "Think. Much water must come through very small space, so it comes fast. If seaweed in the fastest bits have large balloons...?"

Zac could feel himself starting to blush. "The current would rip it out."

"Yes." She hit him with the seaweed. "Plants, animals, rocks all tell you what water will do, if you are smart enough to listen!"

"But I've never seen tides this high before!"

She muttered something exasperated in Hindi. "*Think*, Zac. What makes tides?"

"Umm... the moon's gravitational pull. And the sun's, too, a little."

"But are two moons here. Some of the time, they pull against each other. Cancel each other out."

"Neap tides," Zac said.

"Yes. But now..." she pointed up.

Zac looked up at the sky, and felt his jaw drop. "Wow."

Almost directly above them, the full moons hung in conjunction. The smaller blue Heinlein sat in the center of the larger white disk of Asimov, casting a halo of blue-white light around the moons that made the stars

66

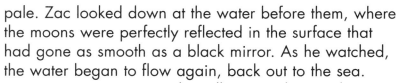

pale. Zac looked down at the water before them, where the moons were perfectly reflected in the surface that had gone as smooth as a black mirror. As he watched, the water began to flow again, back out to the sea.

"Two moons," Lys said. "Pulling together. Make a spring tide. *High* spring tide."

Zac stared up at the moons. Spring tides. When the high tides were higher and the low tides were lower than tides usually went. Which he'd seen when the low tide had exposed Connor's Reef. "I'm an idiot."

"Yes."

"How do you know so much about tides, anyway?"

Lys smiled wistfully. "Mother was smart. Taught me."

"Oh." Zac paused. "What happened to her?"

Lys tucked her knees to her chest and wrapped her arms around them. Zac noticed that her toes were webbed, too — it was actually kinda cute. "Tide was strange, and we hit the Reef. Like you. We both fell in, hurt Her, so She tried to change us both." She drew in a shaking breath. "I was young. My body had not yet begun to change, so it took Her venom well, but Mother..." Zac watched a tear creep down Lys's salt-rimed cheek. "She was not young. Her body finished changing years before, so the venom... killed her."

"I'm sorry," said Zac.

Lys shrugged. "So was She. She found friends for me. Smart creatures in the sea."

But something terrible occurred to Zac. "Lys?" She looked at him. "Will it kill me, too?"

Her eyes unfocused and she cocked her head. He'd seen her do it before, during his talks with her over the months, but this time he could feel an odd buzzing in the back of his mind, like trying to listen to a conversation through a wall. "No," she said. "Your body still changes. You will take the venom, as I did."

"What's it going to do?" he whispered.

Lys held up her hand, fingers splayed. After hesitating briefly, Zac matched his hand to hers. The moonslight shone through her webbing, illuminating the network of tiny blood vessels within it. "Hands change, and feet," she said. "You get stronger. Lungs change, so you don't need to breathe as much. Eyes change so you can see in water. You will start to hear Her." Her eyes met his, and he thought he could see her cheeks grow slightly darker in the moonslight. "You will start to hear me, too."

His face felt suddenly warm. "Was that how She knew where I was?"

"No. She hears us, but cannot find us that way."

"Then how—"

"Water." She pointed at the river, which was picking up speed as the tide turned and the water rushed out to the Bay. "Rivers carry what they know of things that touch them out to sea, where She or one of Her Sisters can taste them. Rain falls and runs into rivers, which run to the sea, and She learns of what the rain touches on land. Or sometimes rain sinks into the ground, to water that lies below the dirt, carrying what it learns with it. In

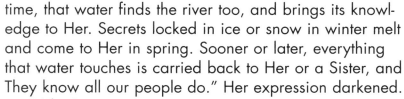

time, that water finds the river too, and brings its knowledge to Her. Secrets locked in ice or snow in winter melt
and come to Her in spring. Sooner or later, everything
that water touches is carried back to Her or a Sister, and
They know all our people do." Her expression darkened.

"What's wrong?"

"They put things into the water."

"Who, the colony?" Zac shook his head. "No, we
learned better when we nearly wrecked Earth. We don't
do that sort of thing anymore. We keep the water pure."

"They *do* put something in the water. In the big metal
places."

He thought for a moment. "Oh, *that*. No, that's just
kinaxin. See, there was this bacteria in the water that
made people kinda sick and dizzy, so they developed
this thing that goes after the bacteria and kills it without
hurting Altaris."

She met his gaze without smiling. "Did they ever ask
what the... bacteria... were for?"

"Well, yeah, but they tested it and stuff. Taking it out
of the water didn't hurt any of the Altaris life."

She shook her head. "They didn't test long enough."

Something in her voice raised the hair on the back of
his neck. "Lys?"

She sat back and stared up at the moons. Zac heard
the buzzing again, louder this time, and he rubbed his
temples as Lys began to speak. "Long ago, in the time of
Her Mother's Mother's Mother, a great rock fell from the
sky. The land shook, the sea rocked, and strange things

stirred from those Deep Places that not even She can know, but they settled quickly and all seemed as it was. For a very long time, nothing happened. Then things began to die. *Everything* began to die."

"The Thanocene extinction..." Zac leaned forward eagerly. "What was it? Dust cloud? Tidal wave? There were all these netbooks—"

"Sickness," she said.

Zac blinked. "A virus?"

Lys nodded. "It grew. Changed. Started with fish, but began to kill everything, above and beneath the sea. But some lived. Some who carried within them a bacteria. Survivors spread. Thrived."

"And so did the bacteria they carried," Zac finished. "So...the bacteria killed the virus?"

She fixed him with her deep, dark eyes. "No. The virus is not dead."

Zac felt his stomach begin to knot. "Then..."

"The bacteria keeps the virus from killing."

"But—" Zac protested feebly. "But they tested *everything* before they built the colony. They would have found something."

"The virus hides well. Sleeps a long time before killing. And then it kills fast." Zac's head buzzed again, and Lys shuddered. "Very fast."

"Maybe we'll be safe. We're not native to the planet, maybe the virus can't adapt —" The look in her eyes stopped him dead. "We already have it, don't we?"

"We walk in rain. Swim in rivers and lakes. Wade in

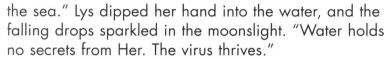

the sea." Lys dipped her hand into the water, and the falling drops sparkled in the moonlight. "Water holds no secrets from Her. The virus thrives."

The gentle night breeze seemed suddenly cold. "And we're killing the bacteria." Zac dropped his head to rest on his knees. "Oh, frack."

"It used to be that She and Her Sisters made guardians of those who hurt them to protect from being hurt again. Now They need more. Need a Voice."

Zac raised his head. "So what, we just walk in to the dispensing stations and say 'scuse us, we know we're out past curfew, but a super-intelligent coral told us to stop cleaning the water?'" He snorted. "They'll never believe us."

"I told Her," Lys said. "So she waited to see if our people would learn on their own. But they don't see. Don't listen. We *must* speak. If they don't believe us, She and the Sisters will act."

Goosebumps dotted Zac's arms. "What will They do?"

She looked at him. "Where does rain come from?"

He turned his gaze to the Bay, and shivered. "From water that evaporates from oceans."

She nodded. "Their venom binds — does not come out when water evaporates, like most things do. If They wished, She and Her Sisters could void venom into the sea."

"And it would get carried up to the clouds when the water evaporates, and fall in the rain over the land. It would get into the drinking water, and people would drink it and start to change. Or die." Zac bit his lip.

"Would She really do that?"

"She does not wish it," Lys said, staring out over the waves. "She hopes we will be enough. There is still a little time. We might still make them stop."

"People won't like the idea of being kinda fluey all the time, Lys."

"Better than kinda dead."

Zac considered that. "Good point."

Lys sighed, and reached beneath the hem of her shirt — Zac blinked at it, and grinned. It was Gan's favorite shirt, from the last *Galactic Scunge* concert. Gan had been absolutely furious when it had gone missing during a class trip to the beach.

Zac stopped smiling when he saw what she had been reaching for.

"She said you wanted this." Lys held out the rock jewel to him. "I found it after I pulled you out. I thought, if it made you go down to the bottom of a narrow estuary when tide was coming in" — she smiled — "it must be important."

His hand trembling, Zac took it from her. "Yeah," he said. "I guess it was." He set the rock jewel in her hair, where it gleamed like a dark star.

"Zac?" she said.

"Yeah?"

"It will be nice." She touched the back of his hand, lightly. "Will be nice to not be alone anymore."

Zac reached out and took her hand in his. Faintly, over the rush of the river and the pounding of the waves, he could hear the throbbing of engines from the rescue crew his mother must have sent out after him. Lys heard it too and tried to stand, but he wouldn't let her go. He had finally realized why, time and time again, he had kept coming back to the Bay since that first day when Lys had pulled him out of the water.

"It's all right," he said. "We can do this. Together."

Lys's eyes were wide, and a little scared. "Promise?"

"I promise." Zac suddenly grinned. "Mom's gonna love you."

To Feast on Royal Jelly

by Francine P. Lewis

"**B**ut I didn't *mean* to do it!"

Rahdavi Hawkes hated sounding like a whining kid, but it was nothing compared to the panic tightening his chest, his uncle's thunderous gaze... or the small, silver creature in his lap, shredding his pants with its claws.

"You should have thought of that before!" Uncle Aka yelled. His brown skin darkened with rage. "You knew those caves were private to the *Sanirtoh mor Sartoh.*"

Although only four of the creatures were in the room, Rah felt as if hundreds of lantern-like alien eyes were burning holes through him. The other people crowding the small office were scientists on his uncle's research team.

The Sannies were four-legged creatures whose skin was armoured with large silvery scales. Their scientific name was *Sartoh placoderma sapiens* — the scaled-skin people. However, the biggest Sannie was barely taller than thirteen-year-old Rah.

"But I can't stay here!" he shouted, struggling to rise from the chair. The little alien, determined to hang onto its perch, dug its claws into his thigh. The scratches stung and he swatted the creature in surprise. It hit the floor squealing, before rolling into a quivering ball.

Hissing in anger, the Sannies flared the large flaps on both sides of their heads like dinner-plate-sized ears, while writhing tentacles shot out of grooves on their upper bodies. This display made them look larger, more dangerous. Rah realised that although they weren't very tall, from the top of its head, to the tip of its segmented tail, the average Sannie was quite long.

"But Mom and Dad are coming back for me in three weeks!" His voice trembled with panic.

"Pick her up!" Uncle Aka ordered and Rah stared at him in confusion. Then he looked down at the silver ball at his feet.

76

"I said to pick... her... up!

Rah crouched to pick up the creature. She shuddered in his nut-brown hands before going still. Curled up, the alien child was smaller than a variable-gravity soccer ball.

"Don't you *ever* strike her again!"

Anger hung like a black cloud between them. Rah had never seen anyone so furious. But as he looked up fearfully at his mother's brother, the anger seemed to flow out of Uncle Aka.

"You can't leave, Rahdavi," he said quietly. "She has imprinted on you. You'll have to remain on Orugoh for at least two standard years. If you leave, she may die."

Rah stared at his uncle incredulously.

"That's ridiculous!" he exploded. "I'm not staying on this dirt-ball for two years with a bunch of Sannies! Mom and Dad are coming for me . . . Aunt Jessie said I didn't even hurt her!"

Uncle Aka's dark eyes flashed with fury again. "No, what you did was worse — you woke her up. She's your responsibility now and I *know* your parents will agree with me! You've been acting like a spoiled brat since you got here. If you hadn't irresponsibly turned off your locator so we couldn't track you, this accident would never have happened! I know you don't care for our work —"

His uncle loomed over him, his tall, black figure suddenly menacing. Rah tried to swallow a lump of fear lodged in his throat.

"But at least you could have shown these people some respect! They are Sanirtoh mor Sartoh and I *never* want to hear you call them Sannies again! From now on, wherever you go — she goes! Now, go to your room and get her to uncurl."

Rah stared at him in humiliated disbelief for a moment, then turned and ran from the office, tears welling up in his eyes. How dare Uncle Aka treat him like this in front of *aliens*! As he pelted down the corridor, even the big, dumb Sannie pack-beasts he passed seemed to stare angrily at him with glowing, golden eyes.

At the fork in the tunnel, Rah stopped. He looked down the right-hand tunnel, which led to the school, recreation facilities and the underground Sannie village. The aliens didn't even live on the surface of their world like normal people! On the planet's surface, temperatures could soar higher than fifty degrees Celsius in the daytime. But life thrived in caves where it was cooler, while underground lakes and rivers provided water.

He started down the dusty tunnel leading to the human living quarters. He'd hated it on arrival two weeks before — he couldn't see the stars. Only the fact that he wouldn't be staying long had made thought of living in a dirty cave bearable. His family's ship, *Banshee*, had been hired to deliver supplies to the Addison star system, located in an area of space frequently raided by pirates. His parents had dropped him off on this dirt-ball where they'd thought he'd be *safe*.

79

Two years? Uncle Aka had to be wrong — he had to
be!

"Rah!"

He turned to face a girl who had lightly tanned skin,
green eyes and curly, brown hair. His cousin, Maida,
was not even thirteen yet, but she was already taller
than he was. She was also the biggest show-off in the
known galaxy.

"What do you want?" he muttered as she ran up to
him.

"To see if you needed any help," she said. Excitement
sparkled in her eyes. "Mom said that you were keeping
her."

"Thanks to you, I don't have a choice!"

"How's this *my* fault?" she demanded. Rah ignored
her and walked away. "Just because I'm better at
physics? It's not *my* fault that you got mad and went into
the hibernation nursery!"

"You solved that last exercise by a fluke — and
nobody explained what would happen if I went in!" he
shouted, turning to face her again.

Maida's emerald eyes flashed as her temper exploded. "*Fluke?*" she screeched. "Fluke! I answered that
problem because I'm better at calculating vectors than
you are. I wasn't stupid enough to forget about gravity
when I did *my* calculations!"

He glared angrily at her. She and the rest of the
physics class had laughed at him that day, when his calculations had thrown his simulated ship off course.

"And you were told about the nurseries," she continued angrily. "Everyone is given the same orientation when they arrive. It's *your* own fault if you didn't pay attention. You were busy acting like you were too good to live down here!" She stomped away, leaving Rah feeling angrier. He had a nagging suspicion that she was right. Entering his quarters, he realised that he didn't like the feeling at all.

The lights came on automatically as the door closed. There were few furnishings — just his bed, storage locker, desk and chair. On the desk, next to his computer was a small holo-cube album. The side of the cube facing him held a hologram of his mother, *Banshee's* captain, standing on the bridge and, although she was smiling for the portrait, her eyes seemed to look at him with disapproval.

Sitting on the edge of the bed, he dropped his guilty gaze to his lap and realised that he didn't have a clue how to convince the creature to uncurl her body. No doubt Maida would have known.

The alien child looked more like a little fat ground-car tire than a ball. Her head and long, flexible torso were tucked in against her belly, while she'd curled her abdomen and tail to lie flat over her spine. Her legs were pulled in close, fitting into grooves made by the curling of her body. Now he could see what the plates on either side of the Sannies' heads were used for, besides making them look big and menacing when they were angry. Curled like this, the plates covered the little creature's head, protecting it on both sides.

Rah wiggled one finger underneath her tail, trying to lift it up. For something so tiny, she was very strong. He could barely pull the tip of her tail away from her body. He was concentrating so hard that he didn't hear the door open.

"You'll never get her to uncurl like that."

He looked up into his Aunt Jessica's laughing eyes. She crossed the room to his bed as the door closed behind her.

"Unless she's relaxed, she won't uncurl," she said, sitting down and putting a container of green stuff on the desk. "It hasn't been a good day, has it?" she said with such understanding that it seemed to draw the tears out of him. She leaned over and drew him into warm hug.

"I didn't mean to wake her," he sobbed. "I just wanted to be alone for a little while."

"I know," his aunt replied, handing him tissues to wipe his eyes. "But it happened and there's no way to undo it. Does she deserve to suffer because of this accident, Rah?"

"No," he whispered. "I don't know what happened! One minute, I was walking —" he wailed. "But I must have stumbled over something, because the next thing I knew, she wouldn't let go!"

"You stumbled over her big brother. She was supposed to imprint on him."

"Uncle used that word – imprint — too," he said in confusion. "But I don't know what it is. He said that she'd imprinted on me and that's why I couldn't leave."

Aunt Jessie nodded understandingly. "Imprinting is when a young organism bonds with an older individual to learn how to act like a member of their species — and for protection," she explained. "The sight, sound, and scent of a parent, for example, helps strengthen the bond. Most baby creatures usually bond with family members during the first few weeks of life —"

Panic flared in Rah's chest again. "But I don't know anything about babies!" he protested. "Much less an *alien* baby!"

Aunt Jessie chuckled. "Sanirtoh mor Sartoh children are different. For them, imprinting happens immediately with the first person they meet after hibernation. Have you noticed that they have two pairs of nostrils?" she asked and he nodded, trying not to sniffle.

"Living in these dark caves, they depend on their sense of smell and excellent hearing rather than vision. In fact, they can tell people apart by scent alone. Inside their noses are special organs that are very sensitive to certain smells. Those organs connect directly to their brains and can cause very rapid changes in behaviour."

"So since I was the first person she smelled, she thinks I'm her guardian," he said grimly. "But do I really have to spend two years baby-sitting her?"

"Yes," she said firmly. "But this little one isn't a baby — " He looked up at her in confusion. "She's sort of a teenager. You will have to teach her how to become an adult." His confusion turned to dismay as she continued.

"Like water-dragons back home, or insects such as bees, moths, and butterflies back on Old Earth, these people undergo metamorphosis."

"You mean they start out like grubs or caterpillars?" he asked in astonishment.

"It's similar," she replied. "But they're not insects. In fact, they're similar to Earth reptiles. However, their babies do look very different from the adults. They are the tiny, brown creatures that you see climbing every-thing."

"They don't have tentacles or scale armour and their legs are short and stumpy," Rah said.

"Exactly," she said smiling. "You'd think they were a different creature entirely."

The door chime interrupted her and Rah called for it to open. Maida watched him warily from the doorway and beside her stood a Sannie who was even shorter than he was.

"Can we come in?" she asked.

"Sure," Rah replied.

As Aunt Jessie opened the container of food, Maida entered diffidently.

She introduced the alien. "This is Ru'Oshid; he's her brother." Rah nodded politely, not knowing what to say — "sorry" didn't seem good enough.

"These little guys have a good way of telling who's a friend," she said, kneeling beside the bed. "Stick your finger under the plate on the side of her head and tickle the hairs in it."

"How does that tell her I'm a friend?" he asked doubtfully as he followed her instructions. It was like putting his finger into a clamp. He bit his lip and tried to wiggle his finger against the short, rough bristles inside the flap.

Maida laughed. She actually looked nice when she laughed, Rah thought. "Because an enemy would try eat her, silly — not tickle her!"

"Her name be Ru'Ainke," Ru'Oshid said slowly.

"Ru'Ainke," Rah repeated softly.

Suddenly, the pressure on his finger eased and the alien child uncurled quickly, stretching her four chubby legs and two pairs of tentacles wide. He burst out laughing and Maida joined him; Ru'Ainke reminded him of a two-year-old yawning after a nap.

She stared up at him with large, golden eyes, nuzzling her cheek against his forearm. He was tongue-tied as he studied her face. Her mouth was beak-like with the upper "lip" curving to a sharp point over her lower jaw. The delicate mesh of scales covering each of her nostrils fluttered gently with every breath, keeping her from breathing in too much dust.

"Sui!" she said. He held his breath, unable to say anything. She sniffed the air deliberately. "Sui?" she repeated.

Maida laughed again. "I think she's hungry."

His aunt pressed a small bowl of food into his hand. Fast as lightening, the little alien flipped over in his lap. Her tentacles shot out and snatched the bowl from him.

Before he could blink, she'd lowered her head into it and was noisily slurping up the food.

"Stop her!" his aunt and cousin shouted in unison and he looked up, startled.

"On the nose, you must tap her," Ru'Oshid added and when Rah hesitated, he crouched down and tapped his little sister on the bridge of her nose between the upper and lower pairs of nostrils. Her head jerked up as if yanked by a string.

"When you want her to stop and pay attention to you, tap her nose and explain what you want," Aunt Jessie said.

To Rah's surprise, Ru'Oshid screeched, "*Screee mavi suiiii veek!*" to which Ru'Ainke repeated, "Sui! Sui!" — a little sulkily, Rah thought.

The older alien tapped her on the nose again, repeated the phrase and plucking one of the child's tentacles from the rim of the bowl with his own, dipped it in the food. The tip of the tiny tentacle flattened to a trowel shape and she slowly lifted a scoop of green mush. Half way to her mouth, the food slipped from the quivering tentacle and landed with a *splat!* on Rah's thigh.

Ru'Ainke gave a frustrated "pleek!" and tried again, this time bringing the bowl closer to her face before taking a scoop. This worked much better, although she had trouble co-ordinating her shaky tentacle to her mouth. But the look in her eyes was proud when she finally managed to get a scoop into her mouth without smearing it all over her face.

Aunt Jessie tapped his shoulder and he met her gaze. "Once Ru'Ainke has finished eating, she'll go to sleep — let her," she said. "It's normal for her to eat and sleep a lot for the next couple of days. However, within the week you'll be responsible for keeping her awake and active, teaching her and making sure that she eats properly — understood?"

Rah nodded "yes" and she continued, "When she falls asleep, come to the infirmary and we'll load a translation program into your neural interface so that you can learn her language. We didn't want to burden your implant with it for such a short stay, but now we should do it as soon as possible."

"I'll be there," Rah promised and his aunt departed. He looked down as Ru'Ainke scooped the last bit of food into her mouth.

Maida took the bowl from the little alien.

"Dad said that Ru'Oshid will come every day to help you," she said, sitting on the bed next to him. "And everyone at school will help too."

Rah eyed her suspiciously. He knew that none of the other children liked him very much, but he hadn't let it bother him since he hadn't expected to stay very long.

"Why would they want to help me?" he demanded.

"Because of her," Maida replied. "I promise that we'll be careful, but we hardly get to meet any children Ru'Ainke's age."

"Why? Your Dad's teams work with them all the time," he said in confusion.

"Even Dad wouldn't go near children her age unless he really had to," she said. "They will bond with us, but it's difficult for us to teach them to become Sanirtoh mor Sartoh adults."

Rah nodded, but he felt sure there was more to it than she was saying. Ru'Ainke sprawled in his lap; her upper eyelids slid over her golden eyes and she fell asleep quickly.

"She is eat full belly," Ru'Oshid said, affectionately stroking her with one tentacle. "Return I when she to eat next food?"

"Yes," Rah replied, feeling suddenly grateful. "Thank you."

After the alien youth left, Rah picked up the little creature and stood. She squirmed a little, but didn't wake up. "I guess I should go to the infirmary now," he said. "Would you mind watching her?"

Maida suddenly looked uncomfortable. "You shouldn't leave her, Rah," she said. "She'll be scared if she can't find you when she wakes up." Before he could protest, she dumped his model starship onto his bed and held out the box. "Here, put her in this and take her with you."

Ru'Oshid showed up every afternoon to help Rah with Ru'Ainke. Within a few days, Rah had come to depend on the alien. Although the doctors had loaded the translation program into his neural interface the week before and a program to help him pronounce the words, he couldn't talk to the kid, much less teach her anything. Rah found it difficult to get his mind — and his mouth — around the squeaks, screeches, and growls of Sannie language, so he didn't bother unless he had to.

On the other hand, Ru'Oshid spoke Standard English fairly well. Rah watched Ru'Ainke sitting on her brother's head, peering over the hood of his carapace. As always, he wondered what they needed him for. *She seems to be doing fine without me*, he thought, as Ru'Oshid stroked her with one tentacle.

The older Sannie was teaching his sister how to tell different kinds of mushrooms apart. Rah looked at the musty-smelling fungi Ru'Oshid had spread out on the cave floor behind the Sannie village. Some, like the bright yellow spheres with the black polka dots were probably dangerous, but the dull brown ones all looked alike. Apparently each smelled different, but he couldn't tell with his human sense of smell.

This whole thing is stupid! Rah told himself resentfully. *He was a starship brat — he didn't belong on some ball of dirt!*

"I'm going to get something to eat," he said abruptly.

"To eat, plenty food I bring," Ru'Oshid said gesturing to the mushrooms proudly.

"I need *human* food," Rah muttered, stalking angrily away... feeling homesick for the stars and for *Banshee*.

Despite her promises, Maida and her friends had

been hardly any help. They all gave the same lame excuse when he asked them to take Ru'Ainke for a couple of minutes so that he could have a little fun; *"She'll get scared if you leave her for too long."* They were willing to help during school hours, but not one of them would give up half an hour of spare time.

A sudden ear-splitting shriek stopped Rah mid-way through the tunnel. He turned in time to see a sinuous, black silhouette rise up from the floor as a flash of silver — Ru'Ainke! — hurtled away from it. Rah raced back without stopping to think. Another flash of silver as Ru'Oshid arrived. The cave snake turned its attack on the Sannie, but he leapt aside and ran up the wall, digging his claws into the packed earth. The snake screamed again as the alien youth scrambled across the roof, frustrating its efforts to reach him.

"Ru'Ainke!" Rah cried. He skidded past the predator and found the trembling silver ball wedged in a crack. As he dug her out, the snake whipped around. Its mouth, full of pointy teeth, gaped wide as it lunged at him. He scrambled backwards, hugging Ru'Ainke tightly to his chest. Ru'Oshid dropped from the ceiling onto the snake's back and plunged his knife into it.

It howled, thrashing violently. Its tail lashed out, smashing into Rah. He rolled out of the way, barely managing to hold on to Ru'Ainke. The snake screamed again as it shook Ru'Oshid off and disappeared into the hole through which it had entered.

The alien youth dragged Rah out of the tunnel as

pounding feet and loud voices converged from all sides. Alien tentacles and human hands worked quickly to fill in the hole.

As Rah fought to catch his breath, he examined the quivering little ball. Ru'Ainke felt cold and clammy; since the first day, she'd never curled up that tightly again.

"What happened?" Rah's aunt demanded, crouching beside them.

"Left her he did and she run to him from me," Ru'Oshid said, golden eyes glowing angrily. "Return back her... to — to *sarrt'ka* now!" he demanded.

"*Sarrt'ka?*" Rah repeated. Suddenly, he knew what Ru'Oshid meant as his implant translated, "*Sarrt'ka* — consciousness."

He wiggled a finger beneath the "ear" flap, feeling for the bristles inside.

"You idiot!" his cousin accused furiously.

"Quiet, Maida," Aunt Jessie said. "It's not his fault that he doesn't know."

Rah looked up as Ru'Ainke uncurled and stretched. "What don't I know?" he asked plaintively as she settled against his chest with a contented little whistle. "What's going on? No one tells me anything, but everyone gets mad at me when I do the wrong thing!"

"You weren't supposed to be here long enough for it to matter," Aunt Jessie said. "And we hoped that Ru'Ainke would be one of few kids who could switch imprinting — so we insisted that Ru'Oshid stay close to you."

"Accept only you, she will," Ru'Oshid said. Rah heard the sadness in the alien's voice. "You be teacher for Ru'Ainke. Wait I must to raise another on the Waking."

"Okay," Rah replied. "I understand that, but I still don't know what's going on."

Aunt Jessie and the other children looked uncomfortable. "I could get Dad," Maida suggested.

But her mother shook her head firmly. "No, he's right," she said. "If he's going to be stuck here for two years, he deserves to know."

Aunt Jessie turned to the alien. "Will you take us to the *srivakka* fields?" she asked. Ru'Oshid nodded and she turned to the other children. "All right, it's time for the rest of you to get back to work." There were a few groans, but they left quickly. "Let's go," she said to Rah.

Rah followed them past the Sannie village, hiking unfamiliar passages for over an hour.

"Where are we going?" he asked again as they trudged through yet another narrow tunnel.

Aunt Jessie stopped abruptly. Rah stumbled into her and stopped open-mouthed as he glimpsed the scene past her shoulder. He walked speechlessly out of the tunnel.

The tunnel opened into a large cavern, bustling with activity. Many Sannies were unloading sacs from their pack-beasts and emptying them into large containers on the sunken floor, but they weren't the ones who had captured his attention.

The cavern roof was alive, teeming with Sannie pack-beasts. They were crawling upside-down, along thick, rope-like cords that threaded through the earth in all directions like haphazard stitches through an enormous quilt. The pack-beasts were picking brown spheres from the cords, tentacles moving efficiently while they hung on with their claws. The Sannies were strapped into harnesses on the animals' backs, holding large sacs open to catch the fruits.

"This is a *srivakka* field," Aunt Jessie said leading him over to one of the storage bins. The group of Sannies unloading the melon-sized fruit from their sacs nodded politely. "The srivakkara trees grow on the surface and their roots produce the spherical organs to store nutrients—"

"Which the Sannies harvest for food," Rah interrupted, impatient with being lectured. "What does that have to do with my leaving Ru'Ainke for a couple of minutes?"

"Don't you ever wonder why we keep correcting you whenever you call them that?" she demanded, green eyes hardening. Her anger startled him.

"I didn't mean anything by it, Aunt Jessie," he said. "But Sanirtoh mor Sartoh is a mouthful to say every time! Besides, everyone back home calls them that — it's just a short form of their name."

"And everyone here uses their full name!"

"So?" he asked, suddenly sulky.

"So, he's not a Sannie —" she replied pointing to Ru'Oshid. She picked up the reins of a pack-beast and it came willingly, stopping a few paces from Rah. Its breath had a strong, unpleasant odour as it brought its huge head close to sniff Ru'Ainke, perched on Rah's shoulder.

"This is a Sannie," Aunt Jessie said quietly.

Rah stared in bewilderment at the creature nuzzling Ru'Ainke. Whipping out its long, purple tongue to lick her, it slobbered Rah's cheek in the process. Moving away from the animal, he wiped off its saliva with the edge of his sleeve.

"This is a *sanir*," she continued and Rah's confusion deepened. "And this is what Ru'Ainke will become if you leave — if she survives after you abandon her."

Rah gaped at the animal in complete shock. He couldn't imagine Ru'Ainke becoming that... a slobbering, brutish animal!

"I don't understand," he said hoarsely. He pulled the little alien into his arms as he backed away from the pack-beast. "Ru'Ainke is a person—not some a-animal!"

"No, Rah, at this stage, she's only a potential person." Aunt Jessie sat on the smooth ledge and patted the rock beside her. Rah sat down and looked at the little being in his care.

"Do you remember studying Old Earth honeybees?" she asked and he nodded, unable to speak with the hard lump in his throat. "Both the Queen and the worker bees are female, yet only the Queen can produce eggs. What makes the difference, Rah?"

"Royal Jelly," he croaked.

"Exactly," his aunt said. "The Queen larva feast on Royal Jelly while the workers are fed honey and pollen. For these people, knowledge and learning — that's their 'Royal Jelly.' It is what transforms them from clever animals into intelligent people. *Sanirtoh mor Sartoh.*"

"Animal-me wake to person-me." Rah translated the name now by accessing his implant. "But that's like saying that chimpanzees can wake up human! Teenagers don't turn into apes if they don't learn!"

Aunt Jessie laughed explosively. "That's a matter of opinion," she said and Rah burst into laughter as well. He'd known a few bullies whom he'd thought acted worse than the apes in the recordings at school.

"Right now, Ru'Ainke only has the ability to become an intelligent person in her society," she said soberly. "Her body has a choice of two pathways, but which pathway is chosen will depend on her brain development over the next two years. And how her brain develops will depend how her mind develops—on what *you* teach her."

She picked up a stone and threw it against the cave wall, dislodging a small cascade of dust. "Teaching a Sanirtoh mor Sartoh child is like throwing that pebble. Learning ignites a spark that releases certain chemicals in a child's brain. These chemicals cause small, but very important changes in specific parts of the brain. However, the changes in brain have big effects on different parts of the child's body. When the *sanir* are

95

threatened, they curl up into balls and wait for the predator to leave or to eat them. They also never grow more than four tentacles."

Because they didn't need them, Rah realised. Unlike Ru'Oshid, who had sixteen tentacles he could use as very nimble fingers, Ru'Ainke only had four — like the *sanir*.

"The Sanirtoh mor Sartoh make tools," Rah thought out loud. He noticed the alert warriors spread throughout the cavern for the first time. "They make weapons and fight the cave snakes — they know how to work in teams and plan strategy."

"Yes," replied Aunt Jessie. "And they have language, the ability to reason and to make decisions. That's what you'll have to teach Ru'Ainke. We can help you, but the responsibility for teaching her will be yours, Rah. That was something we didn't understand when we first came to this world," she said sadly. He looked at her in surprise, but she was staring up at the ceiling.

"That's why your uncle was so angry when you imprinted her. To our shame, many of the *sanir* up there should have become Sanirtoh mor Sartoh. But we interfered where we shouldn't have and by the time we understood the consequences, almost every child we had imprinted had become *sanir*. We don't know why the Sanirtoh mor Sartoh evolved like this, but Ru'Ainke won't learn unless you're with her. It's just the way they are."

Rah looked down at the little silver creature in his lap, shredding his pants again. He had always known he could depend on his parents, on his aunt and uncle, but he'd never known someone who depended on him — whose life and future depended on him.

"Don't worry," Rahdavi Hawkes said at last as he stroked Ru'Ainke's silver cheek. "I will teach her to feast on Royal Jelly."

source material
by Laura Anne Gilman

Each of these haikus is a riddle describing one of
the planets in our solar system. Can you solve them
all? (*Answers on page 100.*)

(ix)
Red dust is dreaming
Hydrogen and oxygen
Solitude is dry.

(viii)
Ancient artefact
Broods upon imagined ills;
A dark-ringed despot.

(vii)
Beyond the rude jokes
A majesty of blue gas;
Georgium Sidus.

(vi)
Sweet, sullen goddess,
Eosphorus and Hesperus
Love's heat lies barren.

(i)
Elemental soup
Chance conspires, dice are thrown –
Humanity dreams.

(ii)
Saturday's child;
Scientific data shows
A visual feast.

(iii)
Quick traveller, you –
Half-hidden by close fire's
Glare – Eccentric beast.

(iv)
Dark in distant cold,
Calculations predicted.
Beyond this, unknown.

(v)
Given name, aware
Perhaps an error was made;
It cries, despairs, fades.

Answers to Planetary Haiku Riddles: (i) Earth, (ii) Saturn, (iii) Mercury, (iv) Neptune, (v) Pluto, (vi) Venus, (vii) Uranus, (viii) Jupiter, (ix) Mars.

Treasures

by Annette Griessman

I awoke suddenly, my heart pounding like something trapped, its thrum coursing in a panic-filled wave outward through my body. My limbs trembled and I fought to still them as I listened. Silence. Nothing but silence.

I took a deep, calming breath. Perhaps it was just a dream. Perhaps I had just imagined that sound of something strange and frightening. I hoped so.

I listened again, raising myself up and blinking against the gloom of night. As I peered over the wall that separated my sleeping place from the rest of my home, a lightning swift motion caught my eye. I froze. I tried to focus on the movement, and was rewarded by a glimpse of something tall and thin, like the reeds that swayed and bobbed at the edge of the great rainbow sea. A second reed-thing darted in through the door.

Both glowed as if lit from the inside with the heat of white-hot fires. I stayed still, fighting the urge to run from the horrors that had entered my home, and I knew — it had not been a dream.

I was not alone. And the intruders were unlike anything I had ever seen.

They were aliens — and I was afraid.

The aliens darted and blurred through the room in a chaotic frenzy. I tried to follow them with just my eyes while keeping the rest of me still, but I found I couldn't. The movements were too quick, too unpredictable. But the motions of the aliens did have an odd, urgent pattern. I sensed they were looking for something in their frantic travels. Then one of them stopped near a rough wall. A hole opened near the alien's top end, and an unbearably high screech filled the room. The other alien stopped as well, its screech joining the first. I sensed triumph in their terrible sounds, and a thin tendril of anger snaked through the fear in my heart. What were they doing? Why had they stopped there? I soon had my answer.

One of the aliens reached out a hot, fragile looking limb slowly enough for me to follow its movement. It reached...reached...and gently lifted a small jewel of radiant blue from its place in the niche in the wall. Another limb reached and lifted a glowing crimson orb from beside it. The brilliant purple and pulsing green gems left behind shifted, rolling in the absence of the others. I worried briefly that heat from the aliens' limbs

would harm the gems, but they appeared untouched. Another screech from one alien, and the blue and crimson jewels disappeared in a blur. The green and purple orbs followed so quickly it was as if they had vanished into the air. But I knew where they were, those jewels. *My* jewels.

The aliens darted from the room in a cacophony of shrill squawks and whistles. And they took my greatest treasures with them.

Rage, black rage filled my being, and I pulled myself down from my place of rest. Footprints littered the floor and trailed out of the door, glowing hotly against the cool stone. What manner of beings were these, I wondered, that could leave the heat of their passage behind? No matter. In a sense, I was grateful. I could not match the speed of the aliens, but they had left me a trail. I moved as fast as I was able, out into the cold, black night. The trail of prints led away to the horizon. My rage lent me speed.

I would have those treasures back, aliens or not. I would get them back or die trying.

It took me hours to follow that glowing trail, a journey that would have tired me any other time. But as the four red moons raced each other across the sky, I felt only strength. Strength and determination. I would not fail, or all was lost.

The trail before me had faded, its heat sucked away by the greedy night air. I strained my eyes to see it and hurry even faster. I must see the trail to its end, to find

the aliens. Surely, they could not go much farther, for
they had almost reached the edge of the sea. A fearful
thought filled my mind. Perhaps the aliens could move as
quickly through the harsh, acid waters as they did over
land. I did not know what they were capable of, after
all. But my treasures...my treasures could not withstand
the waters, and I didn't think the aliens would risk their
precious finds so soon. I imagined my treasures, my very
life, etching away in the waves of corrosive liquid. No.
I pushed the thought firmly from my mind. They would
stop before the sea. They had to.

They did stop before the sea, but they stopped so
near it that the strong sea breeze blew hard against me,
stinging where it touched. I ignored the minor irritation
and blinked at the sight that met my eyes.

Before me towered a mountain. A hot, glowing
mountain.

I had never seen anything like it before.

I had little time to ponder this strange thing, for as I
watched, one of aliens emerged from the mountain,
streaking down a long, sloped ramp. It stopped momen-
tarily on the land, lifting a square blockish thing to its
top end. I squinted as I tried to see the features there
through the almost blinding glow of its heat. Two spots
of color winked on the front of its top end. It held the
blockish thing up to these. Could those be its eyes? I
decided they must be. A larger hole opened below the
eyes, and a rapid puff of hot air escaped into the sea
breeze, followed by another, and another. It was breath-

ing through that hole, although its breaths were very quick. I sucked in air through my mouth and blew it out. My breath did not glow hotly, but it was the same. That large hole must be the alien's mouth — the screeching sounds also came from that place. I wondered if the screeching was the aliens' language. I thought briefly of trying to communicate with them, to ask for my treasures back, but I knew I could not duplicate those sounds, let alone their meanings. I would have to find another way.

The alien in front of the ramp blurred suddenly, disappearing back into the mountain. It returned in the blink of an eye. When it slowed enough for me to see, it pushed a large cube, one that moved on round, rolling circles. It stopped the cube a distance from the mountain and one of the alien's upper limbs lifted the cube's top. The top fell back against the ground with a thump, and the alien rapidly gathered bits of rock and soil and dropped them inside the open cube. I understood that — a storage place. A daring idea began to form in my mind. A wonderful idea. I almost cried aloud at the pleasure of it. My idea might just get my treasures back.

I stood silent and waited for my chance.

When the alien streaked away to the other side of the mountain, I knew my chance had come. I raced forward as fast as I was able, but I was so slow when compared to the aliens. I hoped the alien would stay away until I was ready. My breath, usually so slow and steady, pumped in and out of my lungs like the wind itself, whistling so loudly I feared I would be heard. My heart

pounded with the effort, shaking me with its pulsing.
I had never worked so hard in my life. Of course, I had
never had such a need. My limbs grew numb with the
effort of pulling my body along. But I would not fail.

I pulled myself over the edge of the cube and rolled
inside its dark depths like a rock in a landslide. I had
done it! I curled in on myself as tightly as I could, trying
to blend against the large stones and hunks of soil that
littered the bottom. If the alien looked closely, it would
see me. I closed my eyes and wished upon the cold,
sharp stars overhead that the alien would not look.

And it didn't. When the alien returned, it threw a few
more pieces of rock into the cube, two of them hitting me
along my back. I did not move, and the box closed with
a thud, covering me in darkness. The cube moved suddenly, and swayed with movement. I was being moved
on those round rolling things — and, with luck, I was
being moved into the mountain, the place where my
treasures now surely lay.

The motion of the cube stopped. I stayed still and listened. I could hear the aliens' shrieks and whistles
through the walls of my hiding place. A new, even more
shrill cry cut through the air, loud enough to actually be
painful, and the sounds of the two aliens faded away.
They had moved away from the cube, I reasoned. I had
to act now, for I might not get another chance.

I raised myself up and pushed on the cube's top. It
opened easily at my touch — the material was strong,
but amazingly light. I peered over the edge with wary

eyes. I was now in a large, square room. The smooth walls on all sides glowed with heat, as did the other objects in the room. The heat did not hurt me though, and I pulled myself out of the cube and lowered myself as quietly as I could to the floor. For the room, though hot, was empty.

I tried to make sense of the objects around me. There were more cubes surrounding two curved shapes that rested on four thin leg-like projections. The curved shapes were in the exact center of the room — they seemed important in their placement. They curved in the direction of the largest cube thing in the room, one so large that it had been fastened to the mountain's smooth wall. Maybe my treasures were in that cube. I moved quickly to its side, reaching with questing limbs to find a hole or a niche. A crack ran up the one side of the cube, and down again on the other. I leaned back to better see the crack. If one looked from far away, the crack would form a square. Maybe it would open there, like a lid. I felt a projection near the top of the left crack. I pushed the projection until it gave, and the piece of the cube in front of me fell away, to crash to the floor. I froze in panic at the loud chime of sound that filled the room, but no aliens appeared. I blinked and took a shaky breath, and turned to see what hidden thing I had revealed.

I hoped to see the blue and red and purple and green of my treasures, but found something almost as familiar. Tiny squares of gems, almost like my treasures, flashed and pulsed with light. I reached out with a sense of wonder and revulsion. Had the aliens stolen other beings' treasures and stored them here? If so, I must free them....

I brushed gently against the first square and gasped aloud as the pulses flowed up my limb and exploded in my brain. Images formed of their own accord, images of the aliens and their world and their lives. I felt a moment of panic before I realized I could control the images — change and sort them at will. This was familiar to me — this was how I talked to my treasures. I sorted the images, examining them at length, trying to make sense of the aliens and their mountain.

I held onto an image of the mountain. I asked the square for more information on this mountain, and it complied. Streams of data flashed into me, filling me with knowledge. This was not a mountain, I realized, but a ship. My people had ships for the rainbow sea, but this ship sailed a different place. This ship traveled through the night sky overhead. A *space* ship, said the tiny square.

I grabbed an image of the aliens. *Humans,* said the tiny square. I asked for data on their language and their mission here. A stream of data — in one of the alien's own voice — echoed in my head. I could slow the data so that the shriek of its voice became understandable.

We have landed on Caster IV in an effort to find something to trade. We are in desperate need of fuel — enough to return to Earth. Emily is very sick, and the doctor at Alpha station can't help her. She needs a specialist, and there are none in this sector. We spent our last money at Alpha station. If we don't find some-thing to trade for fuel soon, Emily will die...

The information ended there. The alien's voice was heavy and sad. Emily. What is an Emily? I wondered. The alien talked of Emily as if she was a treasure. Just like my treasures, I thought with a hint of confusion. If they understood about treasures, then why take mine? I asked the tiny square about this. The tiny square, a *data computer* it was named, changed the data stream and gave me an answer.

Great luck! We have found a deposit of high grade lucien crystals. Each crystal is larger than any we've ever seen. Once processed, each crystal will be able to hold a huge amount of data for a data computer. A fortune! The trader at Beta station should pay top dollar. Joseph plans to place a claim on this planetoid, and we can come back for more...once Emily is better, that is. And she will be, now that we have a way to Earth....

I felt a surge of bitter outrage...the lucien crystals, as they called them, were my treasures! They meant to trade my treasures? Unthinkable! Even if their need was great, they had no right. I pulled more information from the computer. No. My treasures weren't these crystals they so sought — they only resembled them. The lucien crystals were not alive. But how to show them their mistake?

I was so caught up with my train of thought that I didn't hear the aliens enter the room behind me. One of them shrilled a warning, and I turned to stare into two pairs of tiny, hot eyes. I froze, not knowing what to do.

The aliens apparently didn't know what to do either. They stood so still I could see every inch of their bodies, unblurred for the first time by any motion. Their two lower limbs were thicker than the two upper ones, and their tops...their *heads,* the data computer supplied, were topped with something that looked like cave moss. They wore a second skin over their primary skin — this second skin held back the heat of their bodies and made those parts it covered glow less brightly. One of the aliens did move, finally, and I lurched back against the wall.

No, it wasn't the alien that moved. It was something in its arms. A small bundle of heat. It turned, and two more eyes stared at me, these eyes large and round. *Emily.* The data computer supplied. *And Joseph and Lora. Humans and their child.*

I quickly asked the data computer how to protect myself against these humans. It showed me how one of my own deep, powerful yells would stun them, make them sleep. I was amazed at their fragility, and lost all of my fear. They could not hurt me, but I could hurt them easily. I accessed more information and realized how I must look to them—a thick-bodied being with a skin that glistened like the lucien crystals they sought. One whose myriad stubby limbs moved with painful slowness as they propelled my faceted body along. I was not longer than one of their upper limbs, and yet almost as thick as their body's middle. I would look like a rock to them, although

I was much heavier, with a denseness no mere rock could match. My eyes would reflect light in such a way as to be almost as blinding to them as their heat was to me. My breath puffed in and out of my cave-like lungs at a rate of about six in one of their hours — if theirs went that slowly they would die of suffocation. And my heart, my massive and powerful heart that filled half of my body, beat with such a strong and ponderous beat that the humans would certainly hear it as its pulse chimed through me. Of course, its beat was only slightly faster than my breathing, and they would not hear it for many more of their minutes.

The human holding the child suddenly streaked into the depths of the ship. Probably to keep the child safe. The other human stayed, its eyes focus on me, its breath puffing out in hot, impossibly quick breaths. Its body heat grew even greater. It appeared to me that the human was heated from a fire inside and its breath was the smoke. The data computer interpreted this reaction as fear. An understandable reaction to an alien invading your home, I thought wryly, recalling my own fear a short time ago. I did not move, but pulled more information from the computer — all that could be learned of these humans. I shoved the data unread into a corner of my mind. I would examine it later at my leisure, it would fill the long winter nights as the four moons ran their lengthy race. Instead, I pulled up the image I desperately longed to find—the image of where my treasures were kept.

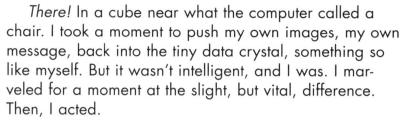

There! In a cube near what the computer called a chair. I took a moment to push my own images, my own message, back into the tiny data crystal, something so like myself. But it wasn't intelligent, and I was. I marveled for a moment at the slight, but vital, difference. Then, I acted.

I let out a yell, the first vocal sound I had made since the aliens had come to my home. The deep sound thrummed out into the air in a wave, knocking over objects in the room, shaking the cubes and chairs. The one remaining human shrieked, its upper limbs darting to grab its hearing organs. It went as limp as a soggy piece of sea weed and fell, crashing to the floor. I hoped it had not been injured. The data computer said the other two humans, Lora and Emily, had also fallen. It reported no injuries, and I was glad. I rushed to the cube that held my treasures, pushing open the lid. Inside the cube, my treasures pulsed in greeting, their own tiny hearts clearly visible through their crystal skin, their tiny, faceted eyes glistening. The fear in those eyes faded as they saw me. I quickly gathered them up and held them close with one of my limbs. They sent me images of happiness and home and I sent them images of love and relief. Together, we moved along the smooth floor and toward the door.

At the door, I paused. The humans were still in need of fuel to take their child home. Their own treasure. I clutched my treasures tight and felt a stab of sympathy. They were in need...how could I not try to help? With a grunt of effort, I broke off one of my back limbs. It tumbled to the floor, its facets glistening dully. It might not be lucien crystal, but perhaps it was close enough. Maybe now they could get home. It was a small price to pay to save a treasure.

I rumbled through the door and into the cool night air. The four racing moons had set, and soon, the long night would end and the sullen, red sun would rise to begin the day. Before then, I would be in my home, my treasures safe once more.

As I moved away from the ship, I wondered what the humans would think of the message I left in their data computer. I might never know.

Greetings, humans. I am Chekek. My people are the Clitch'ikti. I mean you no harm, but you have taken my treasures by mistake. I could not allow you to keep them — they are not yours to trade. I have no ill will to you and wish you well in helping your own treasure, Emily. If you wish to come back some day, I will welcome you.

Even though we are very different, I think we could be friends. For we are alike in one important way...we both love our children.

Our treasures.

114

Defining an Elephant

by Peter Watts

CAPTAIN torched New Zealand today.

It warmed up the orbital lasers and the particle-beam cannons and even a few old-fashioned nukes. We watched, helpless and horrified, as the targeting computers locked on and suddenly *zap*: the East Cape was gone. *Zap*: the Tasman Mountains, burned to the roots. The satellites

dropped their nukes and Stewart Island slagged down to glass before our eyes.

It took a little over thirteen hours. By the time CAPTAIN was finished, twenty-seven complete ecosystems were on fire. Half a million species, fifteen hundred found nowhere else in the world, reduced to ash.

Not to mention the people we lost. Of course, people aren't exactly in short supply, even today. There's still a good six or seven billion of us. It'll be awhile before *we* land on the endangered species list.

About ten months, in fact, according to the latest estimates.

In the meantime CAPTAIN orbits overhead, raining death and destruction onto the world. Every now and then it sends us a report: *Hi there. Thought you'd like to know: everything's going according to plan.*

According to *our* plan. That's the awful thing. It's only doing what we told it to.

Come *one*, come *all*, step right up and see the Fight of the Century.

In this corner, the Champion: *Nature,* twenty-four million species, from the smallest virus right up to giant redwoods and blue whales. In *that* corner, the Challenger: global warming, habitat destruction, sewage, smog, and UV strong enough to peel the tattoos off your butt in thirty seconds flat.

At the sound of the bell, come out swinging.

It was no contest, of course. Nature never had a chance. By the time anybody had reliable figures, almost four hundred species were disappearing every day. We couldn't even *list* them that fast, let alone haul them back from the brink. In thirty years there wasn't going to be much left of the place except rats, seagulls, and nine billion swarming *Homo saps.*

We weren't just talking about losing parrots and poodles and things that looked cute on *Wild Kingdom.* We were talking life-support. Some of those species made the oxygen we breathed. Others ate our wastes and our dead, so we didn't have billions of corpses stinking up the landscape. A lot of them just ate each other, sort of a safety precaution to make sure no one species got out of hand. (Not that that little trick worked in *our* case, mind you...)

We needed them all, like a scuba diver needs an air tank. It was a huge problem just getting anybody to believe that; it was an even bigger one getting them to *do* anything about it. By the time that finally happened — after all the arguments had been won, after everybody finally realised that it was *their* lives on the line — by then, there were only fifteen years left.

How can you save the world in a measly fifteen years? How do you keep tabs on twenty-four million species — or even twelve million, assuming that we'd already killed half of them off? How to you protect all that habitat, keep people from sneaking in and burning

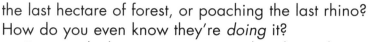

the last hectare of forest, or poaching the last rhino? How do you even know they're *doing* it?

Fortunately there was a system already in place; a veritable feast of hardware left over from fifty years of military-industrial bloat. No self-respecting country goes to war without being able to spy on their enemies. Everyone needs satellites to pick out the other guy's missile silos, listening posts on the seabed to hear hostile submarines on the prowl. They have to be able to snoop in on every square meter of the planet, and they can do it, too; some of those satellites can read the fine print on an insurance waiver from twenty-three thousand kilometers up.

And of course, once the enemy's been found, it has to be dealt with; hence missiles and submarines, orbital lasers and particle-beam cannons.

But by the time all that apocalyptic hardware was ready to go, the War on Dissent was ancient history. Terrorist and Rogue States had vanished along with most of the world's civil rights. Even those nasty little civil disputes in Canada and Africa had blown over. There just weren't any enemies left to try out the new toys on.

This was a real bummer for the military, but it was manna from heaven for us. We swept in and scooped everything up at bargain-basement prices, almost new. Satellites built to spy on enemy airbases could just as easily snoop out poachers and oil spills. Instead of shooting down enemy warplanes and ICBMs, they'd take out illegal logging camps and pirate whaling vessels. It turned out that the NATO system even had a snazzy name: Cognitive Autonomous Planetary Threat-Assessment & Interdiction Network. CAPTAIN, for short.

Naturally, with a name like that, we *had* to put it in charge. We reprogrammed it for good instead of evil and we let it loose with fifteen years left to save the planet.

And it went on to set half the world on fire.

A couple of months ago — before everything went so horribly wrong — Bergmann hauled me into his office. "Perhaps you could explain *this*," he said, pointing at his computer screen.

Bergmann's your basic off-the-shelf military man; he hated it when CAPTAIN got snatched away from the Generals, and he hated having to deal with us tree-hugging environmental eggheads. He knew we were essential to the project — the army doesn't have any theoretical ecologists of its own — so he followed orders like any good soldier.

He didn't like it much, though. He liked us even less.

CAPTAIN was counting species on some test site, assessing biodiversity according to rules we'd pro-grammed into it. The total climbed as I watched — forty species, seventy, a hundred. It levelled out at two hundred eighty three.

"What's the problem?" I asked. "Isn't it picking up all the species?"

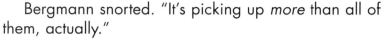

Bergmann snorted. "It's picking up *more* than all of them, actually."

"What do you mean? What's it looking at?"

"You."

"*What?*"

He jerked his head at the ceiling. I looked up: directly overhead, one of CAPTAIN's sensor clusters stared down at me. I took a step to the left. The cluster whirred softly, rotating to keep me in focus.

Bergmann folded his arms. "So maybe you could explain to a simple jarhead like me why the system, using *your* rules, just defined one man as nearly three hundred different *species*."

"Come on, Bergmann. People have a couple hundred kinds of bacteria living on their skin, for starters. A bunch more in the gut. That's all it's counting."

He shook his head. "We already thought of that. The count's still too high."

"Well, I —"

"Fix it," he said. End of interview.

So we fixed it. The problem was simple enough, as it turned out: CAPTAIN was looking within the cells of my own body, and seeing multitudes.

A cell isn't just a cell. It's actually a *colony* of small cells inside a larger one. Some act like batteries, turning chemicals or sunlight into energy. Some keep the genes from getting all tangled up in each other. But it wasn't always thus: a few billion years ago, way before multi-cellular life evolved, the ancestors of those small cells lived free in the primordial goop. One day some larger cell tried to have them for lunch, only to find it couldn't finish the job: it engulfed its prey easily enough, but couldn't digest it afterward. The little cells found they could live quite comfortably inside the thing that had tried to eat them. In fact, *both* parties ultimately found themselves better off than they had been. The host cells could use the chemical energy the little cells put out, while the little cells were comfortably insulated from environmental changes — not to mention other predatory cells that might be a bit better at chewing once they'd swallowed. Everyone was a winner.

They never looked back. We don't even think of the little ones as "cells" any more — we think of them as *parts, organelles,* give them names like "nucleus" and "chloroplast" and "mitochondrion." But they've still got their own genes, left over from the days when they lived on their own. They still reproduce independently. In a way they *are* still individuals, living inside our cells like janitors in a high-rise.

That's what CAPTAIN thought, anyway. It had been counting all those different parts in my cells as separate individuals, even separate *species.* It wasn't even wrong, strictly speaking, just about a billion years out-of-date.

Bergmann wasn't impressed, though. This was the fifth time we'd had to go back and start from scratch.

The problem is, you can't just tell a computer to "go out there and protect the diversity of life." You've got to tell it exactly what life *is*. It's the sort of thing that geek teachers bring up in grade seven biology classes to try and *spark the students' interest.* What is life? they ask, thinking the class is going to get all excited about this garbage. Is a *salt crystal* alive? No? Well, it *grows*, doesn't it? It "eats" ions from the surrounding solution, it incorporates them into its "body", it "grows" — if you break it, it repairs itself — it *heals*, get it? — and a fragment, chipped off the main crystal, will grow on its own, so you could say that's *reproduction* —

Yeah, right. Whatever.

Everybody knows that trees and people are alive. Everybody knows that salt crystals aren't. If that bozo at the front of the class thinks he's going to turn anybody's crank with his lame droning about "living" salt crystals, he's even dumber than he looks.

But the old geezer has a point, you know. There's this list of features that gets trotted out every time you want to describe what "life" is: it breathes, it eats, it grows. It reproduces. The problem is, the list doesn't always work. Viruses *can't* reproduce on their own: they have to hijack the reproductive machinery of some *other* cell to do that for them. And common garden-variety Drano — the stuff you use to unplug toilets — that "breathes," if "breathing" is taking in one kind of gas and expelling another. For every rule, there's an exception — something that obviously *is* alive, even though it doesn't fit the list.

Something else that obviously *isn't*, although it does.

I had this teacher once. "I may not be able to define an elephant," she told me, "but I know one when I see one." Defining life is a lot like defining an elephant. You just sort of, well, know it when you see it.

But try telling that to a machine. You can wave your hands and fudge all you want, but computers are dumb: they just won't get it unless you spell it out *exactly*.

Actually, now that I think about it, there *is* one sure way to tell if something's alive: try to kill it. Only living things can die.

CAPTAIN seems to have figured that much out, anyway.

I'm checking CAPTAIN's satellite feeds right now. I've got access to a million electronic eyes, I can watch the whole world in lovely shades of infrared and ultraviolet. I can see chlorophyll sparkling where plants brighten the landscape; I can see black voids where they've been wiped out.

A lot of those, now. More every day.

I watch as the nukes and the lasers touch down at precise intervals across the planet, turning the world into a piecemeal firestorm. CAPTAIN's hitting eastern Africa today. I try talking to it. If CAPTAIN was human, I'd grab it by the throat and scream, "What in God's name are you *doing*? You're supposed to be *saving* the world!"

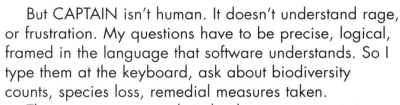

But CAPTAIN isn't human. It doesn't understand rage, or frustration. My questions have to be precise, logical, framed in the language that software understands. So I type them at the keyboard, ask about biodiversity counts, species loss, remedial measures taken.

The computer responds in kind, gives me statistics and diversity indices, estimates that it will achieve the goals we've set it in two years or less. If you translated that response into English, it would be saying "What are you complaining about? I'm doing exactly what you told me to do. I'm protecting the diversity of life."

Another beam lances down from orbit, and Madagascar catches fire.

Back in test mode CAPTAIN was an obedient lapdog. The moment we committed it to a real mission, though, we let it off the leash. It's a military system, after all. Oh, we came in at the last moment and gave it all sorts of nice new mission objectives, but at heart it was always a creature of the battlefield. It was designed to keep going under conditions of total warfare, to interpret any shut-down command as an enemy trick.

Bergmann says there's no way to pull the plug. CAPTAIN's body has a thousand disconnected parts, spread across land and sea and sky. The main components are in orbit, running off onboard reactors or solar power. What are we supposed to do, turn off the sun?

No off switch. I guess it seemed like a good idea at the time.

Okay, so CAPTAIN thought that I was a few hundred different species. Obviously it had a problem with boundaries. It had drawn separate lines around each type of organelle when it should have just drawn a big one around me.

So we went back to basics: many organelles, together, make up a cell; many cells, together, make tissues; tissues make organ systems; and organ systems, taken together, make *one* organism. One. Got that, CAPTAIN? It's the *whole system* that counts, not the crowd of subsystems inside it.

Now do you understand?

CAPTAIN said yes, it did. We gave it some test data to think about overnight, and went home.

Bergmann called me in first thing the next morning. "Okay, what did you geniuses do *this* time? CAPTAIN's claiming that there's only twenty-one species in all of South America."

By the time I got in to work, CAPTAIN couldn't even find that many. It could only count nineteen.

"Oh, man," I groaned. Two more species disappeared as I watched.

"I've really had enough of this," Bergmann said.

"I think I can figure this out. Just listen —"

"*You* listen, mister. Do you have any idea how far this project has fallen behind? We've only got fifteen years to undo two centuries worth of damage, and *you can't even get us past the first step.* At this rate, by the time you figure out how to *define* life, there won't *be* any."

"Look, I think I can —"

"You're *biologists*, for crying out loud! How can you possibly not know what *life* is?"

I tried again. "I think I might know —"

"You're fired. You're all fired." He waved a fax under my nose: authorization from way up the food chain. "We'll do the rest of this ourselves, thank you very much."

"You can't. You don't know how."

Bergmann smiled grimly. "We can't screw up worse than *you* guys."

He was wrong about that, of course.

They brought us back into the loop fast enough when CAPTAIN started torching everything in sight. But now it's too late. The machine is dedicated: it's not going to back off until it's completed the mission.

But I think I know what's going on, now. I know why CAPTAIN's burning the planet down around our ears.

It tried to define the elephant. Only there *is* no elephant.

An elephant is no more "complete" than a cell nucleus, or a heart. So what if it breathes, and breeds, and carries on with all the traditional activities of life? So what if it even has its own genetic code? That means squat: take the nucleus out of the cell and it's toast. Rip the heart from the elephant and both will be dead

127

before they hit the ground. Cut the elephant off from oceanic plankton a thousand miles away, from the oxygen they produce, and it suffocates. Take away the foliage it feeds upon; it starves.

We told CAPTAIN that pieces weren't individuals because they weren't self-sufficient. Now, CAPTAIN is telling us that *nothing* is. It looks for boundaries, and all it finds are connections. If heart and kidneys are just different parts of one system, then elephants and plankton and bamboo must just be parts of a larger one. As is everything else that eats, and everything else that breathes, and so on, and so on.

The longer CAPTAIN thought about it, the fewer individuals it saw. It couldn't tell where one ended and the next began, so it started lumping them all together. It just followed the rules we gave it, and those rules lead to one inevitable conclusion. Ultimately there's only one self-contained, independent living system with a definable edge, anywhere on earth.

Everything. The whole biosphere. It's all just one big organism, as far as CAPTAIN can tell. And since there's only one organism on earth, there can hardly be more than one *species*, either.

Looking back at the records, I can see exactly the point at which CAPTAIN declared war on the world. It fired its first laser when it thought that there were only thirty-two different species on Earth.

I think it's trying to increase that number, the only way it knows how. By spreading fires.

Fire *breathes*, you see. It consumes oxygen, it produces carbon dioxide. It eats too, it consumes everything from wood to flesh. It produces waste in the form of ash and soot. It even reproduces with little airborne spores — "sparks," we call them — that start whole new blazes, completely separate from the parent.

And you know what else is interesting about fire? There are so many different kinds. There's the kind that feeds on dry wood. There's the oil-well fire, and the fireballs that consume flammable gases like methane. There are chemical fires, feeding on sodium and saltpeter. Nuclear fires. Electrical fires. Why, I'll bet there's at least — let's just take a wild guess here — I'll bet there's at least *thirty-three* different species of fire.

CAPTAIN's not trying to destroy life; it's trying to *spread* it. It's just that according to the rules we gave it, fire is alive.

We've got to convince CAPTAIN that it's wrong about that.

I'm not so sure that it is.

More About **Tales from the Wonder Zone**

Illustrated by Jean-Pierre Normand, Edited by Julie E. Czerneda

Stardust
ISBN 1-55244-018-4

> ### *Introduction by Gregory Benford • Original Science Fiction by Alison Baird • Annette Griessman Mark Leslie • Beverley J. Meincke • James Van Pelt*

> **Stardust in Space**—Stardust is also the name of the NASA spacecraft designed to capture samples from a comet and from interstellar dust. Launched February 1999, Stardust returns to Earth January 2006, where its samples will be analyzed for clues to the composition of the early universe.

For more, visit
http://stardust.jpl.nasa.gov/mission/scnow.html

Explorer
ISBN 1-55244-022-2

> ### *Introduction by C.J. Cherryh • Original Science Fiction by Marcel Gagné • James Alan Gardner • Derwin Mak Isaac Szpindel • Pat York*

> **Explorer in Space**—There have been several spacecraft with the name Explorer, starting with the first U.S. satellite, which measured cosmic radiation in 1958, to the most recent, the Galaxy Evolution Explorer. The Galex launched April 28, 2003 and uses its ultraviolet telescope to help study star formation.

For more, visit
http://www.jpl.nasa.gov/missions/current/galex.html

Orbiter
ISBN 1-55244-020-6

Introduction by David Brin • Original Science Fiction by Anne Bishop • Mark Canter • Eric Choi Annette Griessman • Jean-Louis Trudel

Orbiter in Space—Mars Reconnaissance Orbiter launches August 2005. Its powerful camera will show more surface detail than any previous mission. Other instruments will scan underground for water, identify surface minerals, track atmospheric water and dust, and check the daily Martian weather.

For more, visit
visit:http://www.nasa.gov/vision/universe/solarsystem/ mars_reconnaissance_orbiter.html

Odyssey
ISBN 1-55244-080-X

Introduction by Greg Bear • Original Science Fiction by Sarah Jane Elliott • Laura Anne Gilman Annette Griessman • Francine P. Lewis MT O'Shaughnessy • Douglas Smith Peter Watts

Odyssey in Space—Spacecraft Odyssey is part of NASA's on-going exploration of Mars. It is mapping the chemical make-up of the Martian surface, including hydrogen, which shows the presence of water (ice). It is collecting data to help determine radiation-related risks to future human explorers on Mars. Launched April 7, 2001, Odyssey arrived at Mars on October 24, 2001.

For more, visit:
http://mars.jpl.nasa.gov/odyssey/index.html

Open the door and take your first step into ...

Realms of Wonder

Edited by Julie E. Czerneda

The glorious new series of original fantasy stories from some of the world's best and brightest authors.

Summoned to Destiny

It's one thing to deal with magic — quite another to find your fate bound to it.

Fantastic Companions

Whether familiar on the outside, or born in myth, these companions share one thing in common — they are anything but human.

Nothing Less Than Magic

From spellcasters to dollmakers to those whose mere wishes come true, the result is nothing less than magic.

From Legends Born

Whether born in the desert heat or on the Arctic ice, whether told by lamplight, candle, or star, these ancient tales become new in the hands of talented authors.

A Fitzhenry & Whiteside Company

Trifolium Books Inc.